Tucholsky Wagner Zola Scott Sydow Freud Schlegel
Turgenev Wallace Fonatne
Twain Walther von der Vogelweide Fouqué Friedrich II. von Preußen
Weber Freiligrath
Fechner Fichte Weiße Rose von Fallersleben Kant Ernst Frey
Richthofen Frommel
Engels Fielding Hölderlin
Fehrs Faber Flaubert Eichendorff Tacitus Dumas
Eliasberg Ebner Eschenbach
Feuerbach Maximilian I. von Habsburg Fock Zweig
Ewald Eliot
Goethe Vergil
Elisabeth von Österreich London
Mendelssohn Balzac Shakespeare
Lichtenberg Rathenau Dostojewski Ganghofer
Trackl Stevenson Doyle Gjellerup
Mommsen Tolstoi Hambruch
Thoma Lenz Hanrieder Droste-Hülshoff
Dach Verne von Arnim Hägele Hauff Humboldt
Reuter Rousseau Hagen Hauptmann
Karrillon Garschin Gautier
Defoe Baudelaire
Damaschke Descartes Hebbel
Hegel Kussmaul Herder
Wolfram von Eschenbach Dickens Schopenhauer
Bronner Darwin Melville Grimm Jerome Rilke George
Campe Horváth Aristoteles Voltaire Federer Bebel Proust
Bismarck Vigny Barlach Heine Herodot
Gengenbach
Storm Casanova Tersteegen Grillparzer Georgy
Chamberlain Lessing Langbein Gilm Gryphius
Brentano Lafontaine
Strachwitz Claudius Schiller Iffland Sokrates
Katharina II. von Rußland Bellamy Schilling Kralik
Gerstäcker Raabe Gibbon Tschechow
Löns Hesse Hoffmann Gogol Wilde Gleim Vulpius
Luther Heym Hofmannsthal Klee Hölty Morgenstern Goedicke
Roth Heyse Klopstock Kleist
Luxemburg Puschkin Homer Möricke
La Roche Horaz Musil
Machiavelli Kierkegaard Kraft Kraus
Navarra Aurel Musset
Nestroy Marie de France Lamprecht Kind Kirchhoff Hugo Moltke
Nietzsche Nansen Laotse Ipsen Liebknecht
Marx Ringelnatz
von Ossietzky May Lassalle Gorki Klett Leibniz
vom Stein Lawrence Irving
Petalozzi Platon Knigge
Sachs Pückler Michelangelo Kock Kafka
Poe Liebermann Korolenko
de Sade Praetorius Mistral Zetkin

The publishing house tredition has created the series **TREDITION CLASSICS**. It contains classical literature works from over two thousand years. Most of these titles have been out of print and off the bookstore shelves for decades.

The book series is intended to preserve the cultural legacy and to promote the timeless works of classical literature. As a reader of a **TREDITION CLASSICS** book, the reader supports the mission to save many of the amazing works of world literature from oblivion.

The symbol of **TREDITION CLASSICS** is Johannes Gutenberg (1400 – 1468), the inventor of movable type printing.

With the series, tredition intends to make thousands of international literature classics available in printed format again – worldwide.

All books are available at book retailers worldwide in paperback and in hardcover. For more information please visit: www.tredition.com

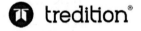

tredition was established in 2006 by Sandra Latusseck and Soenke Schulz. Based in Hamburg, Germany, tredition offers publishing solutions to authors and publishing houses, combined with worldwide distribution of printed and digital book content. tredition is uniquely positioned to enable authors and publishing houses to create books on their own terms and without conventional manufacturing risks.

For more information please visit: www.tredition.com

Pinocchio in Africa

E. Cherubini

Imprint

This book is part of the TREDITION CLASSICS series.

Author: E. Cherubini
Cover design: toepferschumann, Berlin (Germany)

Publisher: tredition GmbH, Hamburg (Germany)
ISBN: 978-3-8495-1773-1

www.tredition.com
www.tredition.de

Copyright:
The content of this book is sourced from the public domain.

The intention of the TREDITION CLASSICS series is to make world literature in the public domain available in printed format. Literary enthusiasts and organizations worldwide have scanned and digitally edited the original texts. tredition has subsequently formatted and redesigned the content into a modern reading layout. Therefore, we cannot guarantee the exact reproduction of the original format of a particular historic edition. Please also note that no modifications have been made to the spelling, therefore it may differ from the orthography used today.

Table of Contents

1. Preface
2. Why Pinocchio Did Not Go To School
3. Pinocchio Assists In Welcoming The Circus
4. Pinocchio Among The Wild Animals
5. Pinocchio Makes Friends With The Wild Animals
6. Pinocchio Determines To Go To Africa
7. Pinocchio In Doubt
8. He Bids Good-by To The Animals
9. Pinocchio Does Not Sleep
10. Pinocchio Eats Dates
11. Pinocchio Lands On A Rock
12. The First Night In Africa
13. Pinocchio Is Well Received
14. Pinocchio Is Arrested
15. Pinocchio's Father
16. Pinocchio Sells Drinking Water
17. A Ride On A Dog's Back
18. The Cave
19. The Caravan
20. The Baby Pulls His Nose
21. Pinocchio Travels With The Caravan
22. He Is Offered For Sale
23. The Bird In The Forest
24. His Adventure With A Lion
25. Pinocchio Is Brought Before The King
26. The Monkeys Stone The Marionette
27. Pinocchio Dreams Again
28. Pinocchio Is Carried Away In An Eggshell
29. Pinocchio Escapes Again
30. Pinocchio Is Swallowed By A Crocodile
31. Pinocchio Is Made Emperor
32. His First Night As Emperor
33. He Sends For The Royal Doctor
34. An Old Story
35. His Duties As Emperor
36. Pinocchio Makes His First Address

37. The Emperor Becomes As Black As A Crow
38. The Hippopotamus Hunt
39. The Emperor Surprises His Subjects By His Wisdom
40. Pinocchio Travels Through The Empire
41. Pinocchio Is Placed In A Cage
42. Pinocchio Performs For The Public
43. Pinocchio Breaks The Cage And Makes His Escape

Preface

Collodi's "Pinocchio" tells the story of a wooden marionette and of his efforts to become a real boy. Although he was kindly treated by the old woodcutter, Geppetto, who had fashioned him out of a piece of kindling wood, he was continually getting into trouble and disgrace. Even Fatina, the Fairy with the Blue Hair, could not at once change an idle, selfish marionette into a studious and reliable boy. His adventures, including his brief transformation into a donkey, give the author an opportunity to teach a needed and wholesome lesson without disagreeable moralizing.

Pinocchio immediately leaped into favor as the hero of Italian juvenile romance. The wooden marionette became a popular subject for the artist's pencil and the storyteller's invention. Brought across the seas, he was welcomed by American children and now appears in a new volume which sets forth his travels in Africa. The lessons underlying his fantastic experiences are clear to the youngest readers but are never allowed to become obtrusive. The amusing illustrations of the original are fully equaled in the present edition, while the whimsical nonsense which delights Italian children has been reproduced as closely as a translation permits.

Why Pinocchio Did Not Go To School

ONE morning Pinocchio slipped out of bed before daybreak. He got up with a great desire to study, a feeling, it must be confessed, which did not often take hold of him. He dipped his wooden head into the cool, refreshing water, puffed very hard, dried himself, jumped up and down to stretch his legs, and in a few moments was seated at his small worktable.

There was his home work for the day, twelve sums, four pages of penmanship, and the fable of "The Dog and the Rabbit" to learn by heart. He began with the fable, reciting it in a loud voice, like the hero in the play: "'A dog was roaming about the fields, when from behind a little hill jumped a rabbit, which had been nibbling the tender grass.'

"Roaming, nibbling. - The teacher says this is beautiful language. Maybe it is; I have nothing to say about that. Well, one more.

"'A dog was roaming about the fields - when he saw - run out - a rabbit which - which - ' I don't know it; let's begin again. 'A dog was running about eating, eating - ' But eating what? Surely he did not eat grass!

"This fable is very hard; I cannot learn it. Well, I never did have much luck with dogs and rabbits! Let me try the sums. Eight and seven, seventeen; and three, nineteen; and six, twenty-three, put don two and carry three. Nine and three, eleven; and four, fourteen; put down the whole number - one, four; total, four hundred thirteen.

"Ah! good! very good! I do not wish to boast, but I have always had a great liking for arithmetic. Now to prove the answer: eight and sever, sixteen; and three, twenty-one; and six, twenty-four; put down four - why! it's wrong! Eight and seven, fourteen; and three, nineteen; and six - wrong again!

"I know what the trouble is; the wind is not in the right quarter to-day for sums. Perhaps it would be better to take a walk in the open."

No sooner said than done. Pinocchio went out into the street and filled his lungs with the fresh morning air."Ah! here, at least, one can breathe. It is a pity that I am beginning to feel hungry! Strange how things go wrong sometimes! Take the lessons - " he went on.

Listen! A noise of creaking wheels, of bells ringing, the voices of people, the cries of animals! Pinocchio stopped short. What could it all mean?

Down the street came a huge wagon drawn by three big mules. Behind it was a long train of men and women dressed in the strangest fashion. Some were on foot, some on horseback, some sat or lay on other wagons larger and heavier than the first. Two Moors, their scarlet turbans blazing in the sun, brought up the rear. With spears at rest and with shields held before them, they rode along, mounted on two snow-white horses.

Pinocchio stood with his mouth open. Only after the two Moors had passed did he discover the fact that he had legs, and that these were following on behind the procession. And he walked, walked, walked, until the carriages and all the people stopped in the big town square. A man with a deep voice began to give orders. In a short time there arose an immense tent, which hid from Pinocchio and the many others who had gathered in the square all those wonderful wagons, horses, mules, and strange people.

It may seem odd, but it is a fact that the school bell began to ring and Pinocchio never heard it!

Pinocchio Assists In Welcoming The Circus

THAT day the school bell rang longer and louder perhaps than it was wont to ring on other days. What of that? From the tent came the loud clanging of hammers, the sounds of instruments, the neighing of horses, the roaring of lions and tigers and panthers, the howling of wolves, the bleating of camels, the screeching of monkeys! Wonderful noises! Who cared for the school bell? Pinocchio? No, not he.

Suddenly there was a loud command. All was still.

The two Moors raised the tent folds with their spears. Out came a crowd of men dressed in all sorts of fine clothes, and women in coats of mail and beautiful cloaks of silk, with splendid diadems on their heads. They were all mounted upon horses covered with rich trappings of red and white.

Out they marched, and behind them came a golden carriage drawn by four white ponies. In it was the big man with the deep voice. There he sat in the beautiful carriage with his dazzling high hat and his tall white collar. He wore a black suit with a pair of high boots. As he rode on he waved his white gloves and bowed right and left. The band with its trumpets and drums and cymbals struck up a stirring march, and a parade such as the townsfolk had never seen before passed out among the crowds that now filled the square.

The marionette could not believe his eyes. He rubbed them to see if he was really awake. He forgot all about his hunger. What did he care for that? The wonders of the whole world were before him.

The parade soon reentered the tent. The two Moors, mounted upon their snow-white horses, again stood at the entrance. Then the director, the man with the loud voice, came out, hat in hand, and began to address the people.

Pinocchio Among The Wild Animals

"LADIES and gentlemen! kind and gentle people! citizens of a great town! officers and soldiers! I wish you all peace, health, and plenty.

"Ladies and gentlemen, first of all, let me make a brief explanation. I am not here for gain. Far be it from me to think of such a thing as money. I travel the world over with my menagerie, which is made up of rare animals brought by me from the heart of Africa. I perform only in large cities. But to-day one of the monkeys in the troupe is fallen seriously ill. It is therefore necessary to make a short stop in order that we may consult with some well-known doctor in this town.

"Profit, therefore, by this chance, ladies and gentlemen, to see wonders which you have never seen before, and which you may never see again. I labor to spread learning, and I work to teach the masses, for I love the common people. Come forward, and I shall be glad to open my menagerie to you. Forward, forward, ladies and gentlemen! two small francs will admit you. Children one franc, yes, only one franc."

Pinocchio, who stood in the front row, and who was ready to take advantage of the kind invitation, felt a sudden shock on hearing these last words. He looked at the director in a dazed fashion, as if to say to him, "What are you talking about? Did you not say that you traveled around the world for - "

Then, as he saw one of the spectators put down a two-franc piece and walk inside, he hung his head and suffered in silence.

Having passed two or three minutes in painful thinking, the forlorn marionette put his hands into his pockets, hoping to find in them a forgotten coin. He found nothing but a few buttons.

He racked his brains to think of some plan whereby he could get the money that was needed. He glanced at his clothes, which he would cheerfully have sold could he have found a buyer. Not knowing what else to do, he walked around the tent like a wolf prowling about the sheepfold.

Around and around he went till he found himself near an old wall which hid him from view. He come nearer the tent and to his joy discovered a tiny hole in the canvas. Here was his chance! He thrust in his thin wooden finger, but seized with a sudden fear lest some hungry lion should see it and bite it off, he hastily tried to pull it out again. In doing this, somehow "r-r-rip" went the canvas, and there was a tear a yard wide. Pinocchio shook with fear. But fear or no fear, there was the hole and beyond - were the wonders of Africa!First an arm, then his head, and then his whole body went into the cage of wild animals! He could not see them, but he heard them, and he was filled with awe. The beasts had seen him. He felt himself grasped at once by the shoulders and by the end of his nose. Two or three voices shouted in his ears, "Who goes there?"

"For pity's sake, Mr. Elephant!" said poor Pinocchio.

"There are no elephants here."

"Pardon, Sir Lion."

"There are no lions here."

"Excuse me, Mr. Tiger."

"There are no tigers."

"Mr. Monkey?"

"No Monkeys.

"Men?"

"There are neither men nor women here; there are only Africans from Africa, who imitate wild beasts for two francs and a half a day."

"But the elephants, where are they?"

"In Africa."

"And the lions?"

"In Africa."

"And the tigers and the monkeys?"

"In Africa. And you, where do you come from? What are you doing in the cage of the wild beasts? Didn't you see what is written over the door? NO ONE ALLOWED TO ENTER."

"I cannot read in the dark," replied Pinocchio, trembling from head to foot; "I am no cat."

At these words everybody began to laugh. Pinocchio felt a little encouraged and murmured to himself, "They seem to be kind people, these wild beasts."

He wanted to say something pleasant to them, but just then the director of the company began to shout at the top of his voice.

Pinocchio Makes Friends With The Wild Animals

COME forward, come forward, ladies and gentlemen! The cost is small and the pleasure is great. The show will last an hour, only one hour. Come forward! See the battle between the terrible lion Zumbo and his wife, the ferocious lioness Zumba. Behold the tiger that wrestles with the polar bear, and the elephant that lifts the whole weight of the tent with his powerful trunk. See the animals feed. Ladies and gentlemen, come forward! Only two francs!"

At these words the men in the cages of the wild animals put horns, sea shells, and whistles to their mouths, and the next moment there came wild roarings and howls and shrieks. It was enough to make one shudder with fear.

Again the director raised his voice: "Come forward, come forward, ladies and gentlemen! two francs; children only one franc."

The music started: Boom! Boom! Boom! Par-ap'-ap'-pa! Boom! Boom! Boom! Par-ap'ap'ap'pa!parap'ap'ap'pa!

One surprise seemed to follow another. Pinocchio longed to enjoy the sights, but how was he to get out of the cage? At length, taking his courage in both hands, he said politely, "Excuse me, gentlemen, but if you have no commands to give me - "

"Not a command!" roughly answered the bearded man who played the lion. "If you do not go away quickly, I will have you eaten up by that large ape behind you."

"But I should be hard to digest," said the marionette.

"Boy, be careful how you talk," exclaimed the same voice.

"I said that your ape would have indigestion if he ate me," replied Pinocchio. "Do you think that I am joking? No, I am in earnest. He really would. I came in here by chance while returning from a walk, and if you will permit me, I will go home to my father who is waiting for me. As you have no orders to give me, many thanks, good-by, and good luck to you."

"Listen, boy," said the large man who took the part of the elephant; "I am very thirsty, and I will give you a fine new penny if you will fill this bucket at the fountain and bring it to me."

"What!" replied Pinocchio, greatly offended; "I am no servant! However this time, merely to please you, I will go." And crawling through the hole by which he had entered, he went out to the fountain and returned in a very short time with the bucket full of water.

"Good boy, good marionette!" said the men as they passed the bucket from one to another.

Pinocchio was happy. Never had he felt so happy as at that moment. "What good people!" he said to himself. "I would gladly stay with them." In the meantime the bucket was emptied, and there were still some who had not had a drink. "I will go and refill it," said the marionette promptly. And without waiting to be asked, he took the bucket and flew to the fountain.

When he returned they flattered him so cleverly with praise and thanks that a strong friendship sprang up between Pinocchio and the wild beasts.

Being a woodenhead he forgot about his father and did not go away as he had intended to do. In fact, he was curious to know something of the history of these people, who were forced to play at being wild animals.

After a moment's silence he turned to the one who had asked him to go for the water and said, "You are from Africa?"

"Yes, I am an African, and all my companions are African."

"How interesting! but pardon me, is Africa a beautiful country?"

"I should say so! A country, my dear boy, full of plenty, where everything is given away free! A country in which at any moment the strangest things may happen. A servant may become a master; a plain citizen may become a king. There are trees, taller than church steeples, with branches touching the ground, so that one may gather sweet fruit without the least trouble. My boy, Africa is a country full of enchanted forests, where the game allows itself to be killed, quartered, and hung; where riches - "

No one knows how far this description would have gone, if at that moment the voice of the director had not been heard. The music had stopped, and the director was talking to the people, who did not seem very willing to part with their money.

Pinocchio Determines To Go To Africa

PINOCCHIO had already resolved to go to Africa to eat of the fruit and to gather riches. He was eager to learn more, and impatient of interruption.

"And the director is an African also?"

"Certainly he is an African."

"And is he very rich?"

"Is he rich? Take my word for it that if he would, he could buy up this whole country."

Pinocchio was struck dumb. Still he wanted to make the men believe that what he had heard was not altogether new to him. "Oh, I know that Africa is a very beautiful country, and I have often planned to go there, and - if I were sure that it would not be too much trouble I would willingly go with you."

"With us? We are not going to Africa."

"What a pity! I thought I could make the journey in your company."

"Are you in earnest?" asked the bearded man. "Do you believe that there is any Africa outside this tent?"

"Tent or no tent, I have decided to go to Africa, and I shall go," boldly replied the marionette.

"I like that youngster," said the man who played the part of a crocodile. "That boy will make his fortune someday."

"Of course I shall!" continued Pinocchio. "I ought to have fifty thousand francs, because I must get a new jacket for my father, who sold his old one to buy me a spelling book. If there is so much gold and silver in Africa, I will fill up a thousand vessels. Is it true that there is a great deal of gold and silver?"

"Did we not tell you so?" replied another voice. "Why, if I had not lost all that I had put in my pockets before leaving Africa, by this time I should have become a prince. And now were it not for the fact that I have promised to stay with these people, to be a panther at two francs and a half a day, I would gladly go along with you."

"Thank you; thank you for your good intentions," answered the marionette. "In case you decide to go with me, I start to-morrow morning at dawn."

"On what steamship?"

"What did you say?" asked Pinocchio.

"On what steamship do you sail?"

"Sail! I am going on foot."

At these words everybody laughed.

"There is little to laugh at, my dear people. If you knew how many miles I have traveled on these legs by day and by night, over land and sea, you would not laugh. What! do you think Fairyland, the country of the Blockheads, and the Island of the Bees are reached in a single stride? I go to Africa, and I go on foot."

"But it is necessary to cross the Mediterranean Sea."

"It will be crossed."

"On foot?"

"Either on foot or on horseback, it matters little. But pardon me, after crossing the Mediterranean Sea, do you reach Africa?"

"Certainly, unless you wish to go by way of the Red Sea."

"The Red Sea? No, truly!"

"Perhaps the route over the Red Sea would be better."

"I do not wish to go near the Red Sea."

"And why?" asked the wolf man, who up to this time had not opened his mouth.

"Why? Why? Because I do not wish to get my clothes dyed; do you understand?"

More laughter greeted these words. Pinocchio's wooden cheeks got very red, and he sputtered: "This is no way to treat a gentleman.

I shall do as I please, and I do not please to enter the Red Sea. That is enough. Now I shall leave you, and he started off.

"Farewell, farewell, marionette!"

"Farewell, you impolite beasts!" Pinocchio wanted to call out, but he did not.

"Come back!" cried the bearded man; "here is the bucket; please fill it once more, for I am still thirsty."

Pinocchio In Doubt

PINOCCHIO went away very angry, vowing that he would avenge himself on all who had laughed at him.

"To begin with," said he, "I intend to make them all die of thirst. If they wait to drink of the water that I bring, they will certainly die." With these thoughts in his mind the marionette started homeward, carrying the bucket on his head.

"The bucket will repay me for all the work I have had put upon me. How unlucky we children are! Wherever we go, there is always something for us to do. To-day I thought I would simply enjoy myself; instead, I have had to carry water for a company of strangers. How absurd! two trips, one after the other, to give drink to people I do not know! And how they drink! they seem to be sponges. For my part they can be thirsty as long as they like. I feel now as if I would never again move a finger for them. I am not going to be laughed at."

As he finished these remarks Pinocchio arrived at the fountain. It was delightful to see the clear water rushing out, but he could not help thinking of those poor creatures who were waiting for him. He had to stop.

"Shall I or shall I not?" he asked himself. "After all, they are good people, who are forced to imitate wild animals; and besides, they have treated me with some kindness. I may as well carry some water to them; a trip more or less makes no difference to me."

He approached the fountain, filled the bucket, and ran down the road.

"Hello within there!" he said in a low voice. "Here is the bucket of water; come and take it, for I am not going in."

"Good marionette," said the beasts, "thank you!"

"Don't mention it," replied Pinocchio, very happy.

"Why will you not come in?"

"It is impossible, thank you. I must go to school."

"Then you are not going to Africa?"

"Who told you that! I am returning to school to bid farewell to my teacher, and to ask him to excuse me for a few days. Then I wish to see my father and ask his permission to go, so that he will not be anxious while I am away."

"Excellent marionette, you will become famous."

"What agreeable people!" thought Pinocchio. "I am sorry to leave them."

"So you really will not come in?"

"No, I have said so before. I must go to school first, and then - "

"But it seems to me rather late for school," said the crocodile man.

"That is true; it is too late for school," replied Pinocchio.

"Well, then, stay a little longer with us, and later you can go home to your father."

Pinocchio thrust his head through the hole and leaped into the tent. The naughty marionette had not the least desire to go to school, and was only too glad of an excuse to watch these strange people.

He Bids Good-by To The Animals

THE show had begun. The director was explaining to the people the wonders of his menagerie.

"Ladies and gentlemen, observe the beauty and the wildness of all these animals, which I have brought from Central Africa. Here they are, inclosed in these many cages, but hidden from your view. Why are they hidden? Because, ladies and gentlemen, you would be frightened at the sight of them, and your peace and health greatly concern me. The first animal which I have the pleasure to present to you is the elephant. Observe, ladies and gentlemen, that small affair which hangs under his nose. With that he builds houses, tills the soil, writes letters, carries trunks, and picks flowers. You can see that the animal was painted from life and placed in this beautiful frame."

The people began to look at one another.

"Now, ladies and gentlemen, let us go on to the next one."

A roar of laughter and jeers arose on all sides. The director saw the unfortunate state of things and began to shout: "Have respect, ladies, for the poor sick monkey I told you of. At this moment she is pressing to her breast for the last time her friendless child."

But not even this was sufficient to calm the crowd, which presently became an infuriated mob. Men and women rushed about the tent, making fierce gestures and heaping abuse upon the director. What an uproar!

In the cage where Pinocchio was, there was no confusion, and the conversation between the marionette and the wild beasts went on without stopping.

"When do you leave for Africa?" Pinocchio was asked.

"Have I not told you? To-morrow morning at daybreak, even if it rains."

"Excellent! But you must carry with you several things which you may need."

"And those are - ?"

"First of all you will need plenty of money."

"That is not lacking," said Pinocchio in his usual airy way.

"Good! Then you should get a rifle."

"What for?"

"To defend yourself against the wild animals."

"Come, come! You don't want me to believe that! I have seen what the wild animals of Africa are!"

"Be careful, marionette. Take a good rifle with you, for one never knows what will happen in Africa."

"But I do not know how to load one."

"Well, then, stay at home. It is folly for you to begin such an undertaking without arms and without knowing how to use them."

"It is you who are foolish. Do not make me angry. When I have decided upon a thing no one can stop me from carrying it out."

"Take care, marionette; you may be sorry."

"Nevertheless I shall go."

"You may find things very unpleasant."

"It is for that very reason that I am going."

"You may never return."

"The good Fairy will protect me."

"Who is the Fairy?"

"How may things you want to know! If you are in need of nothing else, I will bid you all good-by!"

"Farewell, marionette."

"Till we meet again."

"Good-by, blockhead."

"Don't be rude! said Pinocchio, greatly vexed, and out he went.

Pinocchio Does Not Sleep

WHEN Pinocchio arrived at his home he found his father already in bed. Old Geppetto did not earn enough to provide a supper for two. He used to say that he was not hungry, and go to bed. But there was always plenty for Pinocchio. An onion, some beans moistened in water, and a piece of bread which had been left over from the morning, were never missing.

That night Pinocchio found a better meal than usual.

His good father, not having seen his son at the regular dinner hour, knew that the boy would be very hungry. There would have to be something out of the ordinary. He therefore added to the fare some dried fish and a delicious morsel of orange peel. "He will even have fruit," the good man had said to himself, smiling at the joy his dear Pinocchio would feel on seeing himself treated like a man of the world.

The marionette ate his supper with relish, and having finished his meal, went over to his sleeping father and kissed him as a reward for the fish and the orange peel. Pinocchio, to say the least, had a good heart, and would have done anything for his father except study and work.

That night he slept little. Lions, elephants, tigers, panthers, beautiful women dressed in silk and mounted on butterflies as large as eagles, men, in large boots, armed with knives and guns, palaces of silver and gold! All these and a great many more strange sights floated before his dreaming eyes, while he could hear animals roaring, howling, and whistling to the sound of trumpets and drums.

At length the night needed and Pinocchio arose. First of all he went to bid farewell to his friends in the circus, but they were no longer to be found. During the night the director had quietly stolen away with his company.

"A pleasant journey to you!" said Pinocchio, and he began to search the ground for a forgotten piece of gold, or some precious stone which might have fallen from a lady's diadem; but he found nothing.

"What shall I do now? Shall I go to Africa or to school? It might be better to go to school, for the teacher says that I am a little behind in reading, writing, composition, history, geography, and arithmetic. In other subjects I am not so dull. Yes, yes; it will certainly do me more good to go to school. Then I shall be a dunce no longer."

Having made this sensible decision, the marionette started for home with the idea of studying his lessons and of going to school.

Pinocchio Eats Dates

SOON he met a man in a paper hat and a white apron. He was pushing a cart filled with a kind of fruit that Pinocchio had never seen before.

"Dates! dates! fresh dates! sweet dates! real African dates!" came the cry.

"Even he speaks of Africa!" thought Pinocchio. "Africa seems to follow me. But what has Africa to do with dates, and what are these dates? I have never heard of them." The man stopped; Pinocchio stopped also. A lady bought some of the dates, and it happened that one of them fell on the ground. The marionette picked it up and handed it to her.

"Thank you," she said with a smile. "Keep it yourself; you have earned it."

The man with the cart went on, "Dates! dates! fresh dates! sweet dates! real African dates!"

Pinocchio looked after him for a time and then put the date into his mouth. Great Caesar! How delicious! Never before had he tasted anything so sweet. The orange peel was nothing compared with this! What the circus people had told him, then, was really true!

"To Africa I go," he said, "even if I break a leg. What do I care about the Red Sea, the Yellow Sea, the Green, or any other sea? I will go!"

And the rascal, forgetting his home and his father, who at that very moment was waiting to give him his breakfast, set out toward the sea.

As he neared the water he heard a voice call, "Pinocchio! Pinocchio!"

The marionette stopped and looked around, but seeing no one, he went on.

"Pinocchio! Pinocchio! Be careful! You know not what you do!"

"Farewell and many thanks," answered the stubborn marionette, and forthwith stepped into the sea.

"The water is like ice this morning. No wonder it makes me feel cold; but I know how to get rid of a chill. A good swim, and I am as warm as ever." Out shot his arms and he plunged into the water. The journey to Africa had begun.

At noon he still swam on. It grew dark and on he swam. Later the moon arose and grinned at him. He kept on swimming, without a sign of fatigue, of hunger, or of sleepiness. A marionette can do things that would tire a real boy, and to Pinocchio swimming was no task at all.

Pinocchio Lands On A Rock

THE moon grinned again and disappeared behind a cloud. The night grew dark. Pinocchio continued to swim through the black waters. He could see nothing ahead. He swam, swam, swam into the dark. Suddenly he felt something scrape his body, and he gave a start.

"Who goes there?" he cried. No one answered. "Perhaps it is my old friend the shark, who has recognized me," thought he; and he rapidly swam on to get away from the spot which reminded him of that terrible monster.

He had not gone more than fifty yards when his head ran against something rough and hard. "Oh!" cried the marionette, and he raised his hand to the injured part.

Then, as he noticed a large rock standing out of the water, he cried joyously; "I have arrived! I am in Africa!"

He got up on his feet and began to feel of himself all over, his ribs, his stomach, his legs. Everything was in order.

"Nothing broken!" he said. "The rocks on the way have been very kind. However, I hope that day will break soon, for I have no matches, and it seems to me that I am very hungry."

Then he began to move on carefully. First he put down one foot and then the other, and thus crept along till he found a comfortable spot. "I seem to be very tired and sleepy also," he said.

With that, he lay down and went off in to a deep slumber.

When he awoke it was daylight. The sun shone red and hot. There was nothing to be seen but rocks and water.

"Is this Africa?" said the marionette, greatly troubled. "Even at dawn it seems to be very warm. When the sun gets a little higher I am likely to be baked." And he wiped the sweat from his brow on his coat sleeve. Presently clouds began to rise out of the water. They grew darker and darker, and the day, instead of being bright, gradually became gloomy and overcast.

The sun disappeared.

"This is funny!" said Pinocchio. "What jokes the sun plays in these parts! It shines for a while and then disappears."

Poor marionette! It did not occur to him at first that he had slept the whole day, and that instead of the rising he saw the setting of the sun.

The First Night In Africa

"AND now I must pass another night here alone on these bare rocks!" he thought.

The unhappy marionette began to tremble. He tried to walk, but the night was so dark that it was impossible to see where to go. The tears rolled down his wooden cheeks. He thought of his disobedience and of his stubbornness. He remembered the warnings his father had given him, the advice of his teacher, and the kindly words of the good Fairy. He remembered the promises he had made to be good, obedient, and studious. How happy he had been! He recalled the day when his father's face beamed with pleasure at his progress. He saw the happy smile with which his protecting Fairy greeted him. His tears fell fast, and sobs rent his heart.

"If I should die, here in this gloomy place! If I should die of weariness, of hunger, of fear! To die a marionette without having had the happiness of becoming a real boy!"

He wept bitterly, and yet his troubles had scarcely begun. Even while his tears were flowing down his cheeks and into the dark water, he heard prolonged howls. At the same time he saw lights moving to and fro, as if driven by the wind.

"What in the world is this? Who is carrying those lanterns? asked Pinocchio, continuing to sob.

As if in answer to his questions, two lights came down the rocky coast and drew nearer to him.

Along with the lights came the howls, which sounded like those he had heard at the circus, only more natural and terrible.

"I hope this will end well," the marionette said to himself, "but I have some doubt about it."

He threw himself on the ground and tried to hide between the rocks. A minute later and he felt a warm breath on his face. There stood the shadowy form of a hyena, its open mouth ready to devour the marionette at one gulp.

"I am done for!" and Pinocchio shut his eyes and gave a last thought to his dear father and his beloved Fatina. But the beast, after sniffing at him once or twice from head to foot, burst into aloud, howling laugh and walked away. He had no appetite for wooden boys.

"May you never return! said Pinocchio, raising his head a little and straining his eyes to pierce the darkness about him. "Oh, if there were only a tree, or a wall, or anything to climb up on!"The marionette was right in wishing for something to keep him far above the ground. During the whole night these visitors were coming and going. They came around him howling, sniffing, laughing, mocking. As each one ran off, Pinocchio would say, "May you never return!" He lay there shivering in the agony of his terror. If the night had continued much longer, the poor fellow would have died of fright. But the dawn came at last. All these strange night visitors disappeared. Pinocchio tried to get up. He could not move. His legs and arms were stiff. A terrible weakness had seized him, and the world swam around him. Hunger overpowered him. The poor marionette felt that he should surely die. "How terrible," he though, "to die of hunger! What would I not eat! Dry beans and cherry stems would be delicious." He looked eagerly around, but there was not even a cricket or a snail in sight. There was nothing, nothing but rocks.

Suddenly, however, a faint cry came from his parched throat. Was it possible? A few feet from him there was something between the rocks which looked like food. The marionette did not know what it was. He dragged himself along on hands and knees, and commenced to eat it. His nose wished to have nothing to do with it, and would even have drawn back, but the marionette said; "It is necessary to accustom yourself to all things, my friends. One must have patience. Don't be afraid; if I find any roses, I promise to gather them for you."

The nose became quiet, the mouth ate, the hunger was satisfied, and when the meal was finished Pinocchio jumped to his feet and shouted joyously; "I have had my first meal in Africa. Now I must begin my search for wealth." He forgot the night, his father, and Fatina. His only thought was to get farther away from home.

What an easy thing life is to a wooden marionette!

Pinocchio Is Well Received

"FIRST of all," he said, "I must go to the nearest castle I can find. The master will not refuse me shelter and food. Some soup, a leg of roast chicken, and a glass of milk will put me in fine spirits."

The journey across the rocks was full of difficulties, but the marionette overcame them readily, leaping from rock to rock like a goat. He walked, walked, walked! The rocks seemed to have no ending, and the castle, which he imagined he saw in the distance, appeared to be always farther and farther away. As the marionette drew nearer, the towers began to disappear and the walls to crumble. He walked on broken-hearted. Finally he sat down I despair and put his head in his hands. "Farewell, castle! good-by, roast chicken and soup!" He was about to weep again when he saw in the distance a village of great beauty lying at the foot of a gentle slope.

At the sight he gave a cry of joy and without a moment's delay set out in that direction. He leaped over the rocks and bushes, putting to flight several flocks of birds in his haste. Of course only a marionette could go as fast as he did. "How beautiful Africa is! said he. "If I had known this I would have come here long ago."

In a short time he reached the main square of the town. Men, women, and children were lounging about, gossiping, buying, and selling. When they saw the marionette they gathered around him, and many began to shout: "It is Pinocchio! Look, here is Pinocchio! Pinocchio! Pinocchio!"

"Well, this is strange!" said the marionette to himself. "I am known even in Africa. Surely I am a great person."

Like most great men, Pinocchio was annoyed at his noisy reception. In some anger he made his way through the crowd, pushing people right and left with his elbows. He ran down a side street and finally stopped before a restaurant, over which was the sign printed in huge letters:MARIONETTES SERVED HERE."This is what I have been looking for," said Pinocchio, and he went in.

Pinocchio Is Arrested

PINOCCHIO found himself facing a man of about fifty years of age. He was stout and good-natured, and like all good hosts, asked what the gentleman would have to eat. Pinocchio, hearing himself called "gentleman," swelled with pride, and very gravely gave his order. He was served promptly, and devoured everything before him in a way known only to hungry marionettes.

In the meantime the innkeeper eyed his customer from head to foot. He addressed Pinocchio in a very respectful manner, but the marionette gave only short answers. Persons of rank ate here, and to appear like one of them he could not allow himself to waste words on common folk.

Having finished his meal, the marionette asked for something to drink.

"What is this drink called?" he asked, as he put down the glass and thrust his thumb into his vest pocket after the manner of a gentleman.

"Nectar, your excellency."

Upon hearing himself called "excellency" Pinocchio fairly lost his head. He felt a strange lightness in his feet; indeed, he found it hard work to resist the temptation to get up and dance. "I knew that in Africa I should make my fortune," he thought, and called for a box of cigarettes.

Having smoked one of these, the brave Pinocchio arose to go out, when the host handed him a sheet of paper on which was written a row of figures.

"What is this?" asked the marionette.

"The bill, your excellency; the amount of your debt for the dinner."

Pinocchio stroked his wooden chin and looked at the innkeeper in surprise.

"Is there anything astonishing about that, your excellence? Is it not usual in your country to pay for what you eat?"

"It is amazing! I do not know what you mean! What strange custom is this that you speak of?"

"In these parts, your excellency," remarked the innkeeper, "when one eats, one must pay. However, if your lordship has no money, and intends to live at the expense of others, I have a very good remedy. One minute!"

So saying, the man stepped out of the door, uttered a curious sound, and then returned.

Pinocchio lost his courage. He broke down and began to weep. He begged the man to have patience. The first piece of gold he found would pay for the meal. The innkeeper smiled as he said, "I am sorry, but the thing is done."

"What is done?" asked the marionette.

"I have sent for the police."

"The police!" cried the marionette, shaking with fear. "The police! Even in Africa there are policemen? Please, sir, send them back! I do not want to go to prison." All this was useless talk. Two black policemen were already there. Straight toward the marionette they went and asked his name.

"Pinocchio," he answered in a faint voice.

"What is your business?"

"I am a marionette."

"Why have you come to Africa?"

"I will tell you," replied Pinocchio, "You gentlemen must know that my poor father sold his coat to buy me a spelling book, and as I have heard that there is plenty of gold and silver in Africa, I have come here."

"What kind of talk is this?" asked the elder of the two policemen. "No nonsense! Show us your papers."

"What papers! I left all I had at school."

The policemen cut short the marionette's words by taking out their handcuffs and preparing to lead him away to prison. But the innkeeper was a good-hearted man, and he was sorry for the poor blockhead. He begged them to leave Pinocchio in his charge.

"So long as you are satisfied, we are satisfied," said the policemen. "If you wish to give away your food, that is your own affair;" and they went off without saying another word.

Pinocchio's Father

PINOCCHIO blushed with shame.

"Then you are the marionette Pinocchio?"

Upon hearing himself addressed in this familiar way, Pinocchio felt a little annoyed, but recalling the unsettled account, he thought it best to answer politely that he was Pinocchio.

"I am pleased," continued the man; "I am very much pleased, because I knew your father."

"You knew my father?" exclaimed the marionette.

"Certainly I knew him! I was a servant in his house before you were born."

"In my house as a servant? When has father Geppetto had servants?" asked the marionette, his eyes wide with surprise.

"But who said Geppetto? Geppetto is not your father's name."

"Oh, indeed! Well, then, what is his name?"

"Your father's name is not Geppetto, but Collodi. A wonderful man, my boy."

Pinocchio understood less and less. It was strange, he thought, to have come to Africa to learn the story of his family. He listened with astonishment to all that the innkeeper said.

"Remember, however, that even if you are not really the son of the good Geppetto, it does not follow that you should forget the care he has given you. What gratitude have you shown him? You ran away from home without even telling him. Who knows how unhappy the poor old man may be! You never will understand what suffering you cause your parents. Such blockheads as you are not fit to have parents. They work from morning till night so that you may want for nothing, and may grow up to be good and wise men, useful to yourselves, to your family, and to your country. What do you do? Nothing! You are worthless!"

Pinocchio listened very thoughtfully. He had never expected that in Africa he was to hear so many disagreeable truths, and he was on the verge of weeping.

"For your father's sake you have been let off easily. From now on you may regard this as your home. I am not very rich, and I need a boy to help me. You will do. You may as well begin to work at once." And he handed the marionette a large broom.

Pinocchio was vexed at this, but the thought of the black policemen and the unsettled bill cooled his anger, and he swept as well as he knew how. "From a gentleman to a sweeper! What fine progress I have made!" he thought, as the tears rolled down his cheeks.

"If my father were to see me now, or my good Fairy, or my companions at school! What a fine picture I should make!" And he continued to sweep and dust.

Pinocchio Sells Drinking Water

THE time passed quickly. At the dinner hour Pinocchio had a great appetite and ate with much enjoyment. The master praised him highly for the tidy appearance of the store and urged him to keep up his good work.

"At the end of twenty years," he said, "You will have put aside enough to return home, and a little extra money to spend on poor old Geppetto. Now that you have eaten, take this leather bag and fill it with water, which you are to sell about the city. When you return we shall know how much you have made."

The bag was soon strapped on his shoulders and the marionette was shown the door. "Remember," said his master, "a cent a glass!"

Pinocchio set out down the narrow street. He walked on, little caring where he went. His wooden brains were far away. He was grieved. Had the master known just how the marionette felt he would have run after him and at least regained his leather bag.

Pinocchio walked on. He was soon among a hurrying crowd of people. "Can this be Egypt in Africa? I have read about it often."

A Man, wrapped in a white cloak, touched him on the shoulder. Pinocchio did not understand, and started to go on about his business, but the man took him roughly by the nose. Pinocchio shrieked. The crowd stopped. At last, he discovered that the man wanted water. Pinocchio placed the bag on the ground. Then he poured the water into a glass. The man drank, paid, and went his way.

"What a thirst for water Africans have!" thought the marionette, as he remembered his companions of the circus. "I like ices better, and I am going to try to get one with this penny." At once he started off, leaving the leather bag behind.

A Ride On A Dog's Back

A CROWD of boys had by this time gathered in the street. They began, after the manner of boys in nearly every part of the world, to annoy one who was clearly a stranger. They did not know Pinocchio, however, nor the force of his feet and elbows. There came a shower of kicks and punches, and the boys scattered. Away flew Pinocchio. The people were astonished to see those tiny legs fly like the wind. They shouted and ran after him. Pinocchio resolved not to be caught. He turned into a side street that led into the open country. A large dog, stretched out upon the ground, was in his way. Pinocchio measured the distance and leaped.

At that very moment the dog sprang up, and hardly knowing how it happened, Pinocchio found himself astride his back. Barking furiously, the animal shot along like a cannon ball. The poor boy felt sure that he was going to break his neck and prayed for safety. On they rushed. The dog jumped over rocks and ditches as if he had done nothing in all his life but carry marionettes on his back.

"Is it possible that he is a horse-dog?" thought Pinocchio. "If he is, I shall ride him always, and when I return home, I shall present him to my father. My companions will die of envy when they see me riding to school like a gentleman. I shall make him a saddle like those I saw on the circus horses, and a pair of silver stirrups. A saddle is really necessary, because it is very uncomfortable to ride in this way."

The came to a deep gully and the dog prepared to make the leap. Pinocchio muttered to himself: "This is the end. If I cross this in safety, I will surely return home and go to school."

There was a leap, and a plunge into the black, empty air. When he opened his eyes, he found himself lying at the bottom of a precipice in total darkness. How long had he been in the air? The marionette did not know. He remembered only that while flying down he had heard a familiar voice call, "Pinocchio! Pinocchio! Pinocchio!"

"Farewell to the world and to Africa," said the marionette. "Wooden marionettes will never learn. Here I shall stay forever. It serves me right."

The Cave

IF I get out of this prison alive, it will be the greatest wonder I have ever known." Pinocchio sat in the spot where he had fallen. He now began to suffer from thirst. There had been a great deal of excitement, and his throat was parched. He would have given anything for a sip of the water he had so carelessly left in the middle of the street only a little while before.

"I don't want to die here," he said. "I must get up and walk."

So saying, he moved slowly about, groping with his hands and feet as if he were playing blindman's buff. The ground was soft, and the air seemed fresh. In fact, it was not so bad as he had at first thought. Only four things worried him, darkness, hunger, thirst, and fear. Aside from these he was safe and sound.

He had gone but a short distance through the darkness when suddenly he thought he heard a faint murmur. He saw a gleam of light. The blood rushed through his veins. He walked on. The sound became clearer, and the light grew brighter. At length Pinocchio found himself in a cave lighted by soft rays. The murmuring sound was caused by a small stream of water coming out from a high rock and forming a little waterfall. Pinocchio rushed toward the rocks, opened his mouth wide like a funnel, and drank his fill.

"I shall not die of thirst," said the marionette. "Unfortunately, I am still hungry. What a fate is mine! Why can we not live without eating? Some day I am going to find a way. If I succeed, I shall teach the poor people to live without food as I do. How happy they will be!" Meanwhile he looked about for a means of escape. Soon he discovered the hole that lighted the cave, and walked out once more under the open sky.

The Caravan

HE saw nothing but rocks and sand; rocks that shone like mirrors, and sand that burned like fire. He walked on very sadly, without knowing where. Presently he found himself upon a hill, from which he could see a vast plain crossed by a wide highway. A long line of people and camels were on the march, but how strange they looked! They were going along with heads down and feet up. At first the marionette was filled with a strong desire to laugh; then he became frightened and rubbed his eyes, doubting what they told him.

"Am I dreaming?" he said to himself.

The line continued its march, and he distinctly heard the people laugh and joke as they all sat upside down on the backs of the inverted camels.

"I was not prepared for this! What a strange way of traveling they have in Africa! Maybe I too am walking on my head!" and he touched himself to make sure that his head was in its proper place.

Meanwhile the caravan passed on, and Pinocchio stood still, his eyes fixed upon the camels as they disappeared at the turning of the road. The only thing left for him to do was to follow them.

"Either on my head or on my feet I shall surely arrive somewhere! I do not believe that all those people will walk on air forever. Sometime or other they will stop to eat. I shall be there to help them."

As he spoke the marionette started forward, walking rapidly in the hot sun.

The Baby Pulls His Nose

IN half an hour he had caught up with the topsy-turvy caravan. It had stopped at a large well, which was filled with clear, cool water. The people were laughing and talking as if they were at home. They were all as happy as they could be.

Pinocchio could not understand it. Had these people really stood on their heads? What had happened to them? There was something wrong. He had certainly seen them traveling in that strange fashion. However, a marionette who is hungry and thirsty does not worry long about things he cannot explain. He was there, and the people were eating and drinking.

"What a fool I am! If their heads were upside down, they could neither eat nor drink. Surely they will not refuse me a little water, and perhaps as they are familiar with Africa, I may discover in talking with them where the mines of gold and precious stones are to be found."

So saying, Pinocchio moved toward an old man who was sitting with a pipe in his mouth. He had finished his meal and was enjoying a smoke. The marionette took off his hat and said, "Pardon me, sir; what time is it?"

The old man's answer came in a volume of smoke.

"Ask the sun, my boy. He will tell you."

"Thank you!" said Pinocchio, a little taken aback by this reception, and he moved on toward a woman with a baby on her shoulders.

"Madam, will you please tell me if I am on the right road to - "

"The world is wide," broke in the woman.

"And long too," thought the marionette. "How polite these Africans are!"

Of course, the marionette was a stupid fellow. He was a little ashamed to beg for food, and had only asked these questions so that the people might notice him and perhaps offer him food and water.

An ordinary boy would have asked for what he wanted, but the blockhead was too proud.

He was about to go on when the baby began to wave its arms, and to shout, "I want it! I want it!"

Can you guess what it wanted? Pinocchio's nose! The child reached out its hands, and cried and kicked in trying to get hold of it.

The whole caravan looked toward the spot. A group of children gathered about them. Even the camels lifted their heads to see what was the matter. The mother was distressed because the child's screams and kicks continued. She asked Pinocchio to let it touch his nose. His pride was hurt, but thinking it best to humor the child, he went closer and allowed his nose to be touched and squeezed and pulled until the baby was perfectly happy and satisfied. The good woman laughed, and thanked Pinocchio by offering him some bread and milk.

Pinocchio buried his face in the milk and ate the bread. There was no doubt of his hunger. The others offered him fruit and cake. He was pleased. Africa, after all, was a country where one could live. His hunger satisfied, he did what marionettes usually do, talked about himself. In a short time all the people knew who he was and why he had come to Africa. The old man with the pipe asked him, "Who told you that here in Africa there is so much gold?"

"Who told me? He who knows told me!"

"But are you sure that he did not wish to deceive you?"

"Deceive me?" replied the marionette, "My dear sire, to deceive me one must have a good - " and he touched his forehead with his forefinger as much as to say that within lay a great brain. "Before leaving home I studied so much that the teacher feared I should ruin my health."

"Very well," replied the old man, "let us travel together, for we also area in search of gold and precious stones."

Pinocchio's heart beat fast with hope. At last there was some one to help him in his search. He could scarcely control himself enough to say: "Willingly, most willingly! I have no objections. Suit yourselves."

Pinocchio Travels With The Caravan

THE camels, refreshed by the large amount of water they had taken, stood up, proud of their loads. Even the donkey brayed. Yes, there was a donkey! And this fact displeased Pinocchio. He had for a long time felt a great dislike for these animals. In fact, he had once been a donkey, and his dislike was a natural one.

The donkey did not carry any load, and for that reason the marionette was asked to ride on its back. He hesitated. It was stupid to ride a donkey, and he would have preferred to walk, but he did not like to seem rude to the good people, and up he mounted.

They traveled all day along the narrow road which gradually wound around the slope of a mountain. The old man rode by the side of Pinocchio, asking him many questions about the studies he had taken up to prepare himself for this trip to Africa.

The marionette talked a great deal, and as might have been expected, made many blunders. He began to think that his companions were very simple, and that in Africa one could tell any kind of lie without being discovered. He even went so far as to assure the old man that he knew the very spot where they could find gold and diamonds, and ended by saying that within a week they should all be men of great wealth.

"You must walk straight ahead," the saucy marionette was saying, "then to the right, and you will arrive at the bottom of a valley, through which flows a beautiful brook of yellow water. By the side of this brook is a tree, and beneath the tree there is gold in plenty."

The old man was amazed to hear the tales he told. Pinocchio himself felt ashamed of all these lies. He was afraid his nose would grow as it had done one day at home. But no, it was still its natural size!

"Well!" he thought, "if it has not grown longer this time, it will never grow again, no matter how many lies I tell."

He Is Offered For Sale

THEY went on until they met a second caravan resting at a well. Every one admired Pinocchio, and the old man who had him in charge treated him as if he were his own son.

Pinocchio was greatly pleased. Yet to tell the truth he was worried. Suppose they discovered that he had lied, and that he knew nothing about Africa, or the gold, or the diamonds! What would happen then?

The old man was talking to three or four men of the new caravan. Pinocchio did not like their faces. Now and then they looked toward the marionette with open eyes of astonishment.

Pinocchio pricked up his ears to listen to the good things the old man was saying about him. He felt highly flattered on hearing himself praised for his character, his intelligence, and his ability to eat and drink.

Then the men lowered their voices, and the marionette only now and then caught some stray words.

"How much do you want?"

"Come!" replied the good old man, "between us there should not be so much talk. I cannot give him to you unless you give me twenty yards of English calico, thirty yards of iron wire, and four strings of glass beads."

"It is too much. It is too much," replied one.

"They are bargaining for the donkey," said Pinocchio, and he felt sorry for the poor beast.

"I am sorry for you," he went on, addressing the donkey, "because you have made me quite comfortable. Now I must give you up and walk."

"It is too much. It is too much," the men were saying.

"Yes, yes, all you say is very true," spoke one in a high voice, "but, after all, he is made of wood."

"Of wood? Who is made of wood? The donkey?" thought Pinocchio, looking at the animal, which stood still, its ears erect as if it also were listening.

"Here!" put in one of the men, "the bargain is made if you will give him up for an elephant's tooth; if not, let us talk no more of it."

The old man was silent. He looked at the marionette, and then with a sigh which came from his heart he said: "You drive a hard bargain! Add at least the horn of a rhinoceros and let us be done with it."

"Put in the horn!" replied the man, and they shook hands. "You have done well, my friends," the old man said. "That fellow there," - and this time pointed directly at Pinocchio, "that fellow there has some great ideas in his head. He knows a thing or two! He says he knows the exact spot where one may find gold and diamonds."

Pinocchio was thunderstruck! It was he and not the donkey that had been sold.

"Dogs!" he cried, "farewell. I go from you forever." And away he leaped as fast as the north wind. They did not even try to follow him. Who could have caught him

The Bird In The Forest

AFTER two hours of hard running, Pinocchio, still angry at the treatment he had received, came to a forest. "It's better to be a bird in the bushes than a bird in a cage!" he thought.

Although the walk in the forest was refreshing, he began, as usual, to be hungry. The place was very beautiful, but beauty could not satisfy a marionette's appetite. He looked here and there in the hope that he might see trees loaded with the fruit about which the elephant man had spoken. He saw nothing but branches and leaves, leaves and branches. On he walked. Both the forest and his hunger seemed without end.

Fortunately Pinocchio was very strong. Being made of wood, he could endure a great many hardships. He was sure that his good Fairy would come to help him, so he kept on bravely. He had walked a long way before he saw a large tree, bearing fruit that resembled oranges.

"At last!" he cried aloud. The birds flew away at the sound. Pinocchio climbed over the rocks and up the tree as fast as he could.

"I will eat enough to last for a week!" he said, as he thought of the orange peel his father Geppetto had given him for supper.

He picked the largest of the fruit and put it into his mouth. It was as hard as ivory. He pulled out his penknife, with which he used to sharpen his pencil at school. With great difficulty he cut the fruit in two, to find within only a soft, bitter pulp. Then he tried another and another. All were like the first one, and he gave up trying because he was at length convinced that none of the fruit was fit to eat.

Tired and unhappy, with bowed head and dangling arms, he pushed on slowly, stumbling over rocks, and becoming entangled again and again in the briers. He thought sadly of the disappointments he had met with in Africa.

"It is settled. I am to die of hunger. Where are the delicious fruits and the precious stones? Should I not do better to go home and leave the gold and silver to those who want them?"

As he went along, thinking over these things, he noticed ahead of him a bird about the size of a canary, which looked at him as if it longed to console him in his misery. It went on before Pinocchio, flying from one branch to another, stopping when the marionette stopped, and moving every time the marionette moved. Pinocchio said to himself: "Does his dear little bird wish to be eaten? I'll pluck its feathers, stick a twig through it, put it in the sun, and in half an hour it will be cooked and ready to eat."

While the hungry marionette was giving himself up to this thought, the bird began to sing,"Pinocchio, my dear,

If you would honey eat,

Come closer to me here,

And you will find a treat." Imagine Pinocchio's surprise! He approached the little songster and looked up. Sure enough, there on a branch of a great tree was a beehive.

One would think that Pinocchio would at least stop to thank the bird, but not he! Up the tree he went like a squirrel, while the bees buzzed about him angrily. The marionette laughed.

"Sting away! sting away, brave bees! I am a marionette and made of wood. You may sting me as much as you please." He thrust his hand into the hive and drew out a handful of sweet honey.

"This time at least I shall not die of hunger."

His Adventure With A Lion

THE marionette was on the point of filling his mouth a second time, when he heard a frightful roar directly under his feet. The shock almost tumbled him down headfirst. Had he fallen, how unfortunate it would have been! He would have gone straight into the deep mouth of an African lion which was ready to devour him at one gulp.

"Oh, mercy!" cried the marionette. And the lion gave another dreadful roar which seemed to say: "Mercy indeed! I have you now, you little thief."

"Dear lion," pleaded Pinocchio, "have pity on a poor orphan lad who is nearly starving!"

The lion roared still louder. "Who has given you permission to take what belongs to another without having earned it by useful and honest work? In this world he who does not work must starve."

"You are right, my dear lion, you are right. I am ready to pay to the last cent for all the honey I eat, but please don't seem so angry or I shall die of fear."

Then the lion stopped roaring, and sitting down upon the ground, he looked at the marionette as if to say: "Well, what are you going to do about it? Are you coming down or not?"

"Listen, my dear lion," answered Pinocchio; "so long as you stay there, I shall not come down. If you want me to go away and leave the honey, remove yourself a hundred miles or so, and then I will obey you."

The lion did not move.

For almost an hour Pinocchio sat glued to the tree, not daring to eat the honey or to come down to the waiting lion. The hot rays of the sun beat upon him. He felt that he must die, for hunger, fear, and heat seemed ready to destroy him.

"Surely there must be away out of this," he thought. "That lion must have in him some spark of kindness. He has made up his mind to keep me company, and perhaps it is my duty to thank him."

Then the marionette raised his hand to ask permission to speak. It would have been better had he kept still.

At this gesture the lion uttered a roar so loud that it shook the whole forest. He began to lash the ground with his tail, sending up a cloud of dust that nearly choked the marionette, and repeating all the while in lion language, "If you move hand or foot, you will die!"

Pinocchio sat still. Another hour passed in silence. Pinocchio still suffered from the heat and from hunger. Both honey and shade were within easy reach, and he could enjoy neither.

"What an obstinate beast!" he muttered. "How stupid he is to wait there! There is enough room in the forest for us both."

But the lion did not move, and Pinocchio's suffering was great. He was sure now that he was going to die, and he looked sadly at those wooden legs which had carried him through so many adventures. There was the shade, but he could not reach it. There was the honey that must not be touched.

"Eat! eat!" said the honey. "Come! come!" said the shade.

Fortunately a new character now arrived on the scene. A magnificent giraffe came along through the bushes, eating the tender shoots as it approached the spot. Pinocchio saw the giraffe and recognized it at once from a picture of one he had seen in school. The lion saw it also. What should he do? Continue to watch the marionette, or attack and carry off the giraffe? He decided to take the giraffe. As the animal raised its head to bite off the leaves from a tall acacia, the lion leaped at its throat and killed it. Seizing the body in his powerful jaws, the lion disappeared through the forest, and Pinocchio was left behind to have his fill of honey. He ate as he had never eaten before.

When he could eat no longer he came down from the tree, but how strange he felt! His eyes were dim, and his head began to swim, while his legs went here and there in every direction. He could not even talk clearly.

"African honey plays jokes upon those who eat too much of it!" he seemed to hear some one say. He turned to see who it was that had spoken to him, but no one was there. The next moment he fell heavily to the ground as if he had been knocked down with a club.

"That is what happens to greedy boys!" continued the voice of the little bird who had shown him the honey, but Pinocchio lay fast asleep.

Pinocchio Is Brought Before The King

PINOCCHIO had slept for hours when he was aroused by strange sounds. Were these the voices of human beings.

"Yah! Yah! Hoi! Hoi! Uff! Uff!"

What could it possibly be? The marionette opened an eye, but quickly shut it again when he saw a number of coal-black faces turned toward him.

"What do these ugly people want of me?" he asked himself, as he lay there perfectly still.

When Pinocchio next opened his eyes he saw to his great surprise that the men had formed a circle about him. At their chief's command they began to dance. It was all so funny that Pinocchio could hardly keep from laughing. Then the chief made a sign, at which the savages advanced toward the marionette, took him up by his arms and legs, and started away with him.

"This is not so bad," thought the marionette.

After a time his bearers laid him gently upon the ground and commenced to examine him. Pinocchio decided to make believe he was dead.

For that reason he kept his eyes shut tightly and lay still.

Suddenly there was a great noise. He was startled. Opening one eye, he saw approaching a chief followed by a crowd of attendants. Judging from the manner in which the new arrivals were received, they were persons of high rank. At their approach the savages knelt down, raised their hands high in the air, and bent their foreheads to the ground.

A man stepped out from the ranks and came toward Pinocchio. He examined the marionette from head to foot, while all the others looked on in silence.

When the examination was over the marionette hoped to be left in peace, but another approached him and went through the same performance. Then came a third, a fourth, a fifth, and so on.

Pinocchio was somewhat tired of this. As the last one came up he muttered, "Now I shall see what they are going to do with me."

The man who had first examined Pinocchio now approached him again, and calling the bearers, said, in a tongue which, curiously enough, the marionette understood, "Turn the little animal over!"

Upon hearing himself called an animal, Pinocchio was seized with a mad desire to give his tormentor a kick, but he thought better of it.

The bearers advanced, took the marionette by the shoulders, and rolled him over.

"Easy! easy! this bed is not too soft," Pinocchio said to himself.

A second examination followed, and then another command, "Roll him over again!"

"What do you take me for, a top?" muttered the marionette in a burst of rage. But he pricked up his ears when the man who had been rolling him over turned to another and said, "Your majesty!"

Indeed!" thought Pinocchio, "we are not dealing with ordinary persons! We are beginning to know great people. Let me hear what he has to say about me to his black majesty," and the marionette listened with the deepest attention.

"Your majesty, my knowledge of the noble art of cooking assures me that this creature" - and he gave Pinocchio a kick - "is an animal of an extinct race. It has been turned into wood, carried by the water to the beach, and then brought here by the wind."

"Not so bad for a cook," thought Pinocchio. He felt half inclined to strike out and hit the nose of the wise savage, who had again knelt down to examine him.

"Your majesty," continued the cook, "this little animal is dead, because if it were not dead - "

"It would be alive," Pinocchio muttered. "What a beast! How stupid!"

"Because if it were not dead, it would not be so hard. To conclude, had it not been made of wood, I could have cooked it for your majesty's dinner."

Pinocchio said to himself: "Listen to this black rascal! Eaten alive! What kind of country have I fallen into? What vulgar people! It's lucky for me that I am made of wood!"

His majesty then commanded that as the animal was not good to eat it should be buried.

Immediately three or four of the men began to dig a hole, while the unfortunate marionette, half dead with fright, tried to form some plan of escape. The time passed. The hole was dug, and the poor fellow could not think of any plan. Run away! But how? And if they found out that he was alive would he not be cooked and eaten? The marionette did not know what to do.

In the meantime two men had raised him from the ground and stood ready to throw him into the hole. Then in spite of himself, the marionette began to shout at the top of his lungs: "Stop! Stop! I will not be buried alive! Help! Help! My good Fatina! - Fatina! - my Fatina! Help!"At the first shout the two men who were holding him let him fall to the ground and started off in a great fright. All the others followed their example.

"What funny people!" said Pinocchio. "If I had known that they would all run away like this, I should not have been so uneasy. However, I really do not know why I have come here. If I only knew where to find diamonds and gold, it would not be so hard. I might return home to my father, for who knows how much he is suffering because I am not there!"

At that moment he would have given up the whole trip, but he was too stupid to keep an idea in his head for more than a few seconds. Another thought flashed across his mind, and he forgot his poor father.

"If these people run away, it means that they are afraid, and if they are afraid, it means that they have no courage. Now then, I, being very brave, may in a short time come to rule over everything in Africa. Perhaps - who knows! - I may become a king or an emperor!"

Pinocchio, you lazy dreamer, are you never going to learn wisdom? Only a blockhead like you could be so foolish. A wooden emperor, indeed!

The Monkeys Stone The Marionette

FILLED with these hopes and forgetting his fright, Pinocchio set boldly forth without the least alarm at the difficulties of the journey. He was going merrily along, dreaming of all the great things he would do as emperor of Africa, when at a turn in the road there came flying after him a volley of stones. Had any struck him he would have been killed. Astonished and frightened at this strange turn of affairs, he glanced around, but saw no one. He looked up at the trees, and then from right to left, but nobody was in sight.

"This is pleasant!" exclaimed the marionette. "Have those pebbles fallen from the sky?" And he started to go on his way.

He had taken only a few steps, when a second discharge drove him to the shelter of a large tree. Thence he looked carefully in the direction from which the stones continued to come. To his surprise he discovered among the bushes and twigs a large number of monkeys.

"Well! What is this?" cried the marionette. "Those rogues must not be allowed to play such mean tricks. I had better be on my guard."

He picked up a stout stick lying on the ground near by. To his amazement, the monkeys threw away the stones and began to pick up sticks likewise.

"I hope I shall get through this safely!" thought Pinocchio. He raised his stick and threatened the whole army of monkeys.

The monkeys, as if obeying his command, raised their sticks and held them erect, imitating exactly the action of the marionette. Then Pinocchio lowered his stick, and the monkeys lowered theirs. Again Pinocchio lifted his stick as high as he could, and the monkeys raised theirs, holding them stiffly like soldiers on drill.

"Arms rest!" cried Pinocchio.

All the monkeys, imitating the marionette, lowered their sticks in perfect order, just as soldiers do at the officer's command.

"That's a good idea," thought Pinocchio, "I might become the leader of the monkeys, and within a month conquer all Africa." And he laughed at the joke.

The monkeys looked straight at him, standing erect and in line waiting for further orders.

"Ah! you wish to follow me!" said the marionette. "This might suit your taste, but not mine, thank you! I will give you marching orders. Then I shall be left in peace."

Accordingly Pinocchio, who was determined to get away from these annoying beasts, moved two steps forward. The monkeys advanced two steps also. Then he took three steps to the rear, and the monkeys went back three steps.

"At - tention!" and facing about quickly, he started to run. All the monkeys also turned, and began to run in the direction opposite to that taken by the marionette. Pinocchio, laughing at his own cunning, went his way, only now and then turning to watch the dark forms as they disappeared in the distance.

"They all run away in this country," he said to himself, and he too ran on, fearing that the worthy beasts would return for further orders.

Pinocchio Dreams Again

"IF these people are such cowards that they run at the sound of my voice, in a few days I shall be master of all Africa. I shall be a great man. However, this is a country of hunger and thirst and fatigue. I must find a place where I can rest a little before I begin my career of conquest."

Fortune now seemed to favor Pinocchio. Not far off he thought he saw a group of huts at the foot of a hill. He felt that besides getting rest and shelter, he might also find something to eat. Greedy marionette!

As he approached he was struck by the strangeness of these buildings. They looked like little towers topped with domes. He went along wondering what race of people lived in houses built without windows or doors. He saw no one, and he was filled with a sort of fear.

"Shall I go on or not?" he mused. "Perhaps it would be best to call out, Some one will show me where to go for food and shelter."

"Hello there!" he said in a low voice. No one answered.

"Hello there!" repeated the marionette a little louder. But there was no answer.

"They are deaf, or asleep, or dead!" concluded the marionette, after calling out at the top of his voice again and again.

Then he thought it might be a deserted village, and he entered bravely between the towers. There was no one to be seen. As he stretched out his tired limbs on the ground he murmured. "Since it is useless to think of eating, I may at least rest." And in a few minutes he was sound asleep.

He dreamed that he was being pulled along by an army of small insects that resembled ants. It seemed to him that he was making every effort to stop them, but he could not succeed. They dragged and rolled him down a slope toward a frightful precipice, over which he must fall. I even seemed as if they had entered his mouth by hundreds, busying themselves in tearing out his tongue. It served him right, too, because his tongue had made many false promises and caused everybody much suffering."You will never tell any more lies!" the ants seemed to say.

Then the marionette awoke with a struggle and a cry of fear. His dream was a reality. He was covered with ants. He brushed them off his face, his arms, his legs, - in short, his whole body. They had tortured him for four or five hours, and only the fact that he was made of very hard wood had saved his life.

"Thanks to my strong constitution." thought the marionette, "I am as good as new."

Pinocchio Is Carried Away In An Eggshell

PINOCCHIO now found himself in a dense growth of shrubbery which made his progress difficult. He pushed on among the thorny plants. They would have stopped any one but a wooden marionette. His clothes were torn, to be sure, but he did not mind that.

"Soon I shall have a suit that will make me look like a price. Goods of the best quality, and tailoring that has never been equaled! The gold, the silver, and the diamonds must be found." And he went on at a brisk gait as if he had been on the highway.

Trees, shrubs, underbrush, nothing else! The scene would have grown tiresome had it not been for a swarm of butterflies of the most beautiful and brilliant colors. They flew here and there, now letting themselves be carried by the wind, now hovering about in search of the flowers hidden in the thick foliage. From time to time a hare would run between Pinocchio's feet, and after a few bounds would turn sharply around to stare at him with curious eyes, as much as to say that a marionette was a comical sight. Young monkeys peeped through the leaves, laughed at him, and then scampered away.

Pinocchio walked along fearlessly, caring little for what went on around him, and thinking only of the treasures for which he was seeking.

On and on he walked until at length he found himself at the edge of a vast plain. He gave a great sigh of relief. The long march through the woods had tired him. However, he kept his eyes open, now and then looking down at his feet to see if any precious stones were lying about. Presently his attention was drawn to a great hole or nest, in which he saw some white objects shaped like hen's eggs, but considerably larger than his head.

Curious to see whether or not he could lift one, Pinocchio approached the nest. Just then he heard a frightful noise behind him.

Turning quickly, the marionette saw a huge bird running toward him. The next moment a powerful push sent him head over heels upon one of the eggs! As he fell he heard a loud crash, and at almost the same instant found himself carried through the air. What had befallen him?

Of course, the hole was the nest of an ostrich. Enraged at the sight of the broken egg, the fierce bird had seized in its powerful beak that part of the shell into which the unfortunate marionette had fallen, and was now rushing across the plain with the swiftness of an express train.

The marionette screamed in terror, and with the stick which he still held in his hand rained blows upon the bird's long neck. But the blows had no effect whatever. The furious creature ran and ran and ran. Pinocchio, gasping for breath, was certain that his end was near.

The mad race lasted for hours. Suddenly the marionette was thrown into a muddy pool, in which he sank up to his neck like a frog. Having no desire to be suffocated in the mud, he raised his head a little, although he did not try to climb out. What he saw surprised him beyond measure.

Pinocchio Escapes Again

HIS ostrich was no longer alone. There stood another. The new arrival, somewhat smaller, but uglier and even more ferocious than the first, moved cautiously, ready for fight. Suddenly Pinocchio saw the gleam of a knife, and an instant later the ostrich that had carried him thus far fell to the ground, wounded to death. The marionette could not understand how it was possible for a bird to carry a knife hidden beneath its wings and to make use of it. Yet the thing had happened right before his eyes; there was no doubt about it.

While seeking an explanation for his very strange incident, he saw the victorious ostrich draw first one arm, then the other, from beneath its feathers, and finally take off its beak and place it upon the ground. The second ostrich was a man.

Pinocchio now began to understand what had happened, and to hate the trickster who had put on the feathers of an ostrich, in order to attack and kill the poor creature that lay there breathing its last.

The man approached the dying ostrich and tried to lift the huge bird to his shoulders, but in spite of his great strength he failed. Then looking about in search of help, he saw the marionette, whose head was out of the water, and signaled to him to come ashore. Pinocchio would have refused, but there was the knife lying on the ground, and there was the man. He decided to obey.

He came out of the pond as best he could, and the ugly black man began to laugh. He laughed and laughed until he was able to stand no longer, and could only throw himself upon the ground, where he lay, breathless and weak. The marionette, seeing this, said to himself: "If I do not escape now, it will be my own fault. My dear legs, it is no dishonor to run when you must!" and he went on at a gallop toward a hill which could be seen a short distance away.

"May you die of laughing, you villain!" he cried as he ran.

Presently he was somewhat alarmed to discover that the man was running after him. Feeling sure, however, that he could easily outrun his pursuer, he halted a moment, as if waiting for him. The man was hurrying on, thinking that the boy could go no farther, when the saucy marionette, putting his hand to his mouth, shouted "Cuckoo!" Then at a pace swifter than the wind he set off once more, pausing now and again to call out, "Cuckoo! Cuckoo!"

Pinocchio had nearly reached the top of the hill, and the man was halfway up, when a loud roar made them both stop. Turning around, they saw that a lion was carrying off the dead ostrich. At that, the hunter thrust his fingers into his curly hair, and without paying further attention to the marionette, started off to regain the knife, which was still lying where it had fallen.

"Tit for tat," Pinocchio shouted after him, and went on up the hill.

Pinocchio Is Swallowed By A Crocodile

WHEN Pinocchio reached the top of the hill he looked around for a place where he could rest. He thought of the lion that had carried off the ostrich, and he did not like the idea of meeting him. Fortunately there were no signs of life, but neither was there any place where he could sit down in comfort. Sand and rocks, rocks and sand were everywhere. In the distance he saw water.

"At any rate," he said, "I shall at least be able to wash myself;" and he turned his footsteps toward the water.

He arrived before long at the water's edge. How fresh and clean it was! He was so dusty and tired that there was only one thing to do, take a bath! When Pinocchio decided upon a course of action he did not hesitate. In an instant he was undressed.

As he started toward the water a voice cried, "Pinocchio! Pinocchio!"

"Oh, let Pinocchio alone!" the marionette said, and leaped into the air.

Horrors! As he came flying down, a green mass rose to the surface of the river. It was a crocodile! Pinocchio saw it and shuddered, but there was no time to cry out. Down, down he went into that open mouth! But wooden marionettes are always fortunate. The crocodile's throat was so wide that Pinocchio slipped into the stomach of the creature with great ease. Not even a scratch! As he was accustomed to being under water and inside the bodies of animals, he was not at all frightened. In fact, when he noticed that he was being carried down to the bottom of the river, where it was cool and refreshing, he uttered no word of complaint, but rather enjoyed the experience. The crocodile crawled in to a cave, and prepared to digest the marionette at its leisure. Pinocchio was naturally annoyed at this and began to kick and squirm about.

At first this did not seem to cause any ill effects, but Pinocchio kicked and struggled until the poor reptile could not help wondering what the trouble was, and began to twist and shake its whole body. Pinocchio did not stop. Presently the crocodile decided to return to the surface and deposit the marionette upon the bank. Pinocchio desired nothing better. As soon as he saw a ray of light he became very quiet. The crocodile, now that the trouble seemed over, was about to return to its cave, but it had made this plan without consulting our wooden marionette.

"Suppose I let the beast carry me a short distance! I can make it throw me upon the bank later as well as now! It may carry me to some place where - enough, I am going to try it! A green ship, without sails, without engines, and without a crew, is not to be found every day. Boo! boo! boo!" muttered the marionette.

The crocodile, frightened at the strange noises inside its body, began to swim with all its strength. It swam and swam and swam! When it slowed up the marionette continued, "Boo! boo! boo!" and the crocodile went on faster than ever.

The poor creature became thoroughly exhausted, and fairly wept with anger and fright, but the strange voice went on without ceasing.

At last, growing desperate, the crocodile stopped, opened its huge jaws, and with a great effort sent the marionette flying through the air to the bank of the river; then it disappeared in the deep water.

"Pleasant trip home! Remember me to everybody!" cried Pinocchio as he leaped about joyously.

Pinocchio Is Made Emperor

FINDING himself without any clothes, the marionette began to think of his condition. To go back and search for his suit was out of the question. To go about in that state did not seem proper, although he knew that the Africans in general were dressed in the same fashion.

Finally he decided to make himself a suit of leaves. There were some beautiful ones near by that were just suited to the purpose. He knew how to go to work, for at home he had often made clothes out of shavings and twigs. He set about his task at once and in a short time had made a garment that reached from his waist down to his knees. He was busy selecting the leaves for a coat when he happened to raise his eyes, and saw a crowd of men and women rushing about as if either very happy or frantic with terror.

"Lunatics!" he murmured, and went on with his work, for he disliked to be seen half-dressed. All at once the marionette heard a hissing, humming sound. A cloud of arrows fell around him. He was amazed and terrified, not by the arrows, for what harm could arrows do to him? - but by the idea that this meant more trouble for Pinocchio.

"So long as they shoot, I fear nothing; but if they try to capture me, I may have to jump into the river and take to my green ship."

The arrows continued to fall like hailstones on his shoulders, on his breast, on his arms and legs; but of course they dropped to the ground without doing any harm. The natives were astonished. They looked at one another in blank surprise.

Pinocchio, weary of the game, turned in anger toward them and shouted: "Give up shooting, stupid ones! Do you not see that you are wasting your time?" They had already perceived that this was true, and they stopped shooting. A group braver than the rest now approached the marionette and surrounded him. One of them shouted, "Hoa! Hoi! Hoi!"

"Pinocchio!" answered the marionette.

"Yah! Yah! Yah!"

"Pinocchio!" the boy repeated. "Are you deaf?"

Then they began to shout in chorus: "Yah! Yah! Hoi! Hoi! Uff! Uff! Uff!"

And Pinocchio replied: "Yah! Yah! Hoi! Hoi! Uff! Uff! Uff!

This conversation soon began to be wearisome, and Pinocchio tried to escape. It was too late. The Africans, quick as a flash, closed in about him and, seizing him by the legs, raised him from the ground, shouting: "Long live our emperor, Pinocchio the First! Long live our emperor, Pinocchio!"

Pinocchio had never dreamed of such a welcome.

"Long live Pinocchio!"

"Ah! at last! I knew that in Africa my greatness would be recognized. Now I shall be revenged on you, my dear restaurant-keeper, and on you, dear policemen, who wanted to arrest me. Old man, you who wanted to sell me for a rhinoceros horn, now it is my turn!" Thus thought Pinocchio.

This was his first triumph. Flocking like ravens, his African subjects came to render homage to the new emperor, who was carried aloft on willing shoulders. As he passed, all bowed to the ground and then followed in his train. Such a multitude joined the procession that it looked, from a distance, like a vast blot of ink. They went along singing the praises of Pinocchio the First, Emperor and King of all the African kings, sent from heaven to earth to replace the late emperor, who had died the preceding day.

As they marched a great chorus chanted: "He was to come forth from the mouth of a crocodile! He was to remain unharmed by poisoned arrows! He was to have a wooden head! Long live our emperor, Pinocchio the First! Hurrah! hurrah! hurrah!"

"They shot poisoned arrows at me!" thought the marionette. "That is the way they treated their future king. Lucky for me that I am made of wood, very hard wood too! How fortunate that I came to Africa as a marionette! If I had been a real boy, there would be little to say about Pinocchio now."

His First Night As Emperor

PINOCCHIO, his heart filled with joy, entered the capital of his new empire amid the shouts of the people who crowded the streets. The children, rolling on the ground in glee, raised such a dust that one could hardly see.

Forward, forward, they marched through the streets until the main square was reached. The city was not a large city. Pinocchio was a little disappointed. The houses were only huts plastered with mud. The streets and even the main square were dirty.

"I will change all that," Pinocchio gravely said to himself. "I will build a new city." To the marionette such a task appeared to be an easy matter.

In a corner of the square stood a hut somewhat larger than the others. This was the royal palace. Pinocchio was not pleased. The king of all Africa should have something far better than this. However, he thought it would not do, just at this time, to utter any words of complaint.

In the huts about the palace lived the people of the court. These were the advisers and the leaders, who stood ready to carry out the commands of his majesty.

Like many another in such a situation, Pinocchio did nothing but bow his head in agreement with everything that was said to him. This greatly pleased the people of the court and gained for him their admiration and applause. They called him Pinocchio the Wise!

Night came and all the people withdrew. The emperor was left alone with his servant, a gigantic African, who invited his majesty to pass into the royal bedchamber.

The furniture was as simple as the palace itself. A string, stretched across the room, served as a clothes-hanger. The bed was a leopard's skin that swung from four poles. Having displayed with pride these equipments, the servant pointed to a frying pan, which was to be struck with a wooden mallet in case his majesty desired to call the attendants. He then withdrew from the chamber, bowing as he went out.

"Apparently they do not eat here," said the marionette. "Maybe these people think that an emperor is never hungry! However, night passes quickly." Then he undressed himself and lay down. He was quite tired out, and he felt sure that in a few moments he should be fast asleep. But soon he began to roll and toss about uneasily. The bed was hard and uncomfortable. He opened his eyes. There was a spider crawling over him, and he shivered. Other spiders, as large as crabs, were creeping quietly over the ground and the walls as if this was their home and not the king's!

There was one spider twice as large as the others. Surely he was the head of that large family. He fixed his fiery eyes upon the marionette and spoke in the voice of the Talking Cricket: "Where have you come from - fool that you are? What do you think you have gained by becoming the emperor of these people? Return to your home, and be content to be a boy like the rest, and to learn a trade by which you may help your father and be happy yourself."

Upon hearing these familiar words the marionette wanted to beat the pan and call for help, but, he reflected, this would show that he lacked courage and might lower him in the eyes of his subjects. So he endured his fate, thinking: "A night soon passes. Tomorrow night I will have a sentinel on guard." And he drew himself up, mallet in hand, ready to fight the spiders if they came too near him. All was still, and Pinocchio tried a second time to close his eyes to sleep.

"Buzz! buzz! buzz!"

The place swarmed with flies.

"Zz! zz! Zeeee, zeeee, smm, zmmm!"

Out in the night frogs croaked, birds cried, wild animals howled.

"What a place to sleep in!" whined the poor emperor, flinging himself about on his hard bed.

Then he thought of his own small cot, neat and clean, in which he had so often peacefully slept and dreamed pleasant dreams. It will not seem strange that Pinocchio wished that he were at home again, instead of being a king in Africa.

Pinocchio the First, Emperor and King of all the African kings, passed a very wretched night. He felt hot and feverish, and he was afraid that he was going to die before morning came.

He Sends For The Royal Doctor

PINOCCHIO presently became very anxious about his health. He was sure that the night's troubles had brought on a high fever, and this, of course, would keep him from attending to affairs of state. At dawn, therefore, Pinocchio the First rapped the pan and sent for the doctor of the court. He was an old man, with a long white beard. Having listened to the emperor's lament, the doctor drew out a string of beads from his breast, threw them on the floor, and examined them closely, all the time murmuring strange words. Then he began to count the beads. At the end of a quarter of an hour he said that his royal majesty was in excellent health and need not worry.

The marionette's rage knew no bounds, but it would not do to complain at the very beginning of his career. He thanked the worthy doctor therefore, and dismissed him with a polite nod of the head. Then he again rapped furiously on the pan. There promptly appeared eight or ten servants, who first knelt down at the foot of the imperial bed, and then advancing with every sign of respect, raised his majesty gently, and placed him upon a panther's skin that was stretched upon the floor. Pinocchio allowed them to proceed, until they began to cover his body with oil. At this, he asked why they anointed him in such a manner.

"To make you clean, your majesty," answered the servants, very respectfully.

"Fine cleaning!" thought the marionette. "How are my face and hands to get washed this morning? Never mind. Let us see what comes next."

This first operation ended, Pinocchio the First was made to sit cross-legged to have his hair combed. His attendants covered his hair with a purple cream and then sprinkled over it a golden powder.

Pinocchio's joy upon seeing that glittering substance knew no bounds, but he overheard one of the servants say in a melancholy undertone: "What a pity his majesty has not a black complexion such as we have! What a pity! What a pity!"

The marionette was moved to the bottom of his heart, and he was about to say, "You may be sure, my dear subjects, I shall do the best I can to become black," when he heard footsteps approach.

An Old Story

THE grand chamberlain was announced.

This grave person had come to inquire about his majesty's health, and at the same time to notify him that the council had fixed the day for the coronation.

Pinocchio the First listened and approved. The grand chamberlain, very much pleased with his reception, made a deep bow, and was apparently about to retire, when, as if he had forgotten something important, he approached the emperor again and said with great respect, "Your majesty, in the name of the council I must announce to you that to-morrow the lessons begin."

"What lessons?" said the marionette, feeling a chill creep down his back.

"Ah! I will explain," the chamberlain replied meekly. "The things that your majesty must do to straighten out the affairs of state are very simple. Only two words are needed, 'Yes' and 'No!' But to say 'Yes' or 'No' at the proper time requires at least one month of instruction. To make sure that you learn, there will be, twice each day, a punishment of ten lashes of the whip, to be given your majesty on whatever part of the body you may desire. However, in view of the present wisdom of your majesty, the council has agreed that the lessons and the lashings may be delayed till the end of the month, if your majesty so decides."

Pinocchio had listened gloomily until he heard the last words, and then he came near laughing outright. He kept his face very serious, however, and bowed his head as if in deep thought. After a long silence he said, "I have decided to leave the lessons till the end of the month."

The grand chamberlain made a profound bow and went out.

The servants went away also, and Pinocchio, finding himself alone, jumped about in great glee.

"Compulsory fiddlesticks! What blockheads they were to think that I was going to start to-day! At the end of the month, perhaps! There are still thirty days, and in thirty days what may not happen!"

And he looked about quite satisfied with himself. He was sure that everything would go well during his stay in Africa.

"If they sprinkled my hair with gold, they will fill my pockets with money," he thought. And then to his surprise he found that the suit they had put on him had no pockets.

"I shall make pockets as soon as I have time," he said, and striking the pan, ordered the servants to bring in his breakfast.

His Duties As Emperor

PINOCCHIO was served with a piece of elephant's nose, cooked in a highly seasoned sauce. How he twisted his face and ground his teeth! Evidently the meal was not to his liking. He would have preferred some fish, some grapes, and a dozen figs, but he was ashamed to ask for these dainties. He gulped down the food as best he could, and drank from a gourd a great deal of water; then he felt more comfortable.

His ministers had been waiting some time, and Pinocchio did not think it wise to prolong his first meal. With a truly stately stride he entered the audience chamber.

Pinocchio the First, Emperor and King of all Africa, felt it to be his first duty to express his gratitude for the magnificent reception that had been given to him. The ministers made an equally polite response.

Persons of rank now came to pay homage to the new king. Among them were great chiefs of tribes, princes, and kings of the neighboring states. Pinocchio received them all with much pomp. This sort of thing was at first very pleasing to him. But day after day the visitors and the feasts continued. As Pinocchio was the host, he had to eat with all these newcomers. He became very stout, and his jaws ached from so much chewing. Eating was becoming a burden to him. He even longed for the days when he had gone hungry. However, one must take things as they come and be ready to suffer for the good of one's country.

One day there came to the court three kings, the most powerful within a range of a thousand miles. The first was clad in a white skirt, and a military coat which he had bought from an English captain. He came with his head uncovered and a high hat in his hand. The second wore an old helmet on the back of his head. The third carried a clumsy sword in one hand and in the other a broken umbrella.

They bowed to the ground very respectfully, and then each in turn slapped Pinocchio in the face.

The marionette, who did not expect this sort of greeting, was about to express his anger, when the master of ceremonies whispered in his ear that such a greeting was given only to great people.

"When in Rome, do as the Romans do," thought Pinocchio, and he smiled at the visitors.

Dinner was then announced. Pinocchio felt sick at the thought of eating again. It was the fifth time that day, and the sun was still high in the sky, but of course it was not proper to dismiss three kings without having feasted them.

They went out to the dining room, which was under a tree. Beneath the branches were more than a thousand people. They all sat on the ground, and were waited upon by tall young men, who carried around large plates of meat. The three kings gave themselves up to the joys of eating. They took their food in their hands and swallowed it without even stopping to chew it. Each man ate enough to satisfy a score of ordinary people, for African kings are great eaters. The poor marionette tried to eat as much as the others did. He felt that his reputation depended upon it. How he suffered!

At sunset, when all had satisfied their hunger, there was placed before them a strange-looking affair with a long tube fastened to it. A disagreeable smoke came out of it.

"What new thing is this?" thought the marionette, but he did not say a word, for by this time he had learned that an emperor must appear to know everything.

The matter, however, was quickly made clear. The outfit was a huge pipe, with a long mouthpiece. The master of ceremonies presented the mouthpiece to the emperor and asked him to have the kindness to smoke.

"What blockheads!" the marionette muttered to himself. "I never smoke anything but the finest cigars!"

Still, he considered it wise to make no objections. He puffed twice on the pipe stem, and then passed it to the king that sat at his right hand.

The king drew a mouthful and then passed the pipe to his next neighbor. Thus the pipe moved along in regular order until it came back to Pinocchio. Poor Pinocchio! he was already feeling a little queer after his first attempt, and did not enjoy the idea of smoking again; but he knew that he must live up to the reputation of a great emperor. Accordingly he bravely took the pipe and puffed half a dozen times.

Alas! It would have been better for him had he not tried it again! He was wretchedly sick. His head swam dizzily, and the sweat stood out on his forehead. He tried to hide his feelings by talking, but what he said was sheer nonsense.

"When I was king in my own country, the Talking Cricket told me - because my feet burned - that the alphabet had been swallowed by the cat - that was hung to a tree by a dog - that was owned by the director of the circus."

He gazed around him, frightened at his own words, but he saw the flushed faces of the people and heard them whisper: "The sea talks - " "The sun is filled with stars - " "The tiger laughs - " "The summer is red - " and similar phrases equally sensible.

"What is the matter with everybody?" thought the marionette, as he looked about, and saw one of the kings asleep on the ground beside him. Other forms were stretched out around them. Even as he looked, Pinocchio the First, Emperor and King of all Africa, fell over on his wooden nose, and he too was soon fast asleep.

Pinocchio Makes His First Address

THE next day was a splendid one. The sky was a clear blue, the earth was green and fresh. Thousands upon thousands shouted with joy. Pinocchio was to be crowned king and emperor.

He had carefully prepared the royal address, and came proudly forward mounted upon a large elephant, towering above his people. The trumpets sounded, the drums beat, the children rolled on the ground. At a signal from the master of ceremonies all was still. Even the birds ceased to sing. A troop of monkeys, leaping about in the trees, paused to listen. The emperor spoke as follows:

"Ministers of Africa, officers of the army, chiefs and underchiefs, servants and slaves, men, women, and children, all, beloved subjects, listen to the voice of your emperor!" - and Pinocchio looked around at the multitude.

"We, Pinocchio the First, speak to you, and bring to you the word of peace and of love. A new day is about to open to you. Rejoice, O people! We have concluded to bring happiness to every heart and riches to every home. We shall not reveal all the plans which, in time, we hope to see carried out. We shall begin very modestly. Our first gift to you, O people, is Time. Time is very valuable. We have a great deal of it in store. Our kingdom is rich in Time; therefore we have decreed to give each of you as much Time as you want. How can we be more generous!

"Behold the bright sun in the clear blue sky! There is not its equal anywhere else in the world. Kings are proud of it. We, your emperor and ruler, have decreed that every one of you, our faithful subjects, may enjoy the sunlight free of any charge, without tax or duty. Can we be more unselfish?

"You hear the song of the birds, the voices of the animals, the rustling of the leaves in the wind! These also we give you to enjoy at your leisure, and without expense.

"There is one thing, however, that needs our special notice, and this we shall now bring to your attention. Remember, we shall enforce with all our power this law we are about to propose."

Here Pinocchio placed his hand upon his breast and looked toward the sky.

"We will never introduce into our kingdom that shameful system which brings sorrow to many countries known to us. We speak of the horrible scheme called Compulsory Education! What a disgrace it is, beloved subjects, to see so many bright, intelligent children seated for hours and hours before books which ruin their eyesight! The eye is a precious jewel, and it is improved, not by books, but by looking here and there, above and below, everywhere and anywhere, as the butterflies and the birds do. Let us teach our children as nature teaches us. Let us burn our books and our schools. Do not drive our dear little ones to silly words and cruel numbers. It makes our heart bleed to see parents call their children from some pleasant game and shut them up in ugly schoolrooms."

At this point Pinocchio was so moved that he had to stop. He looked around at the many mothers, and saw them wipe the tears from their eyes. Proud of the impression his words had made on these kind hearts, he went on in a tone so pathetic that it touched even the elephant which carried him. "These are gentle tears, dear subjects, and they show how noble are your hearts. You love your children. We ourselves will never see them suffer. No, a thousand times no! We are not so cruel as to tear you away from your dear ones. They may continue to roll upon the grass, free as the birds that fly. They are free to hunt for crickets, to steal birds' nests, to bite and to kick each other, to run and play in the fields and woods with the monkeys.

"We consider these exercises very necessary, and whenever the grave affairs of the state will permit we will visit you and encourage these sports. You perceive that in this matter you owe much to your emperor, who was made to go to school, and who saw the evils of education. Alas! too many of his young companions were completely ruined so far as their eyes and brains were concerned.

"Officers and soldiers, ministers of the crown, beloved subjects, we, Pinocchio the First, Emperor and King, ask you to shout with all the breath in your lungs: 'Down with Compulsory Education! Down with the school!'"

A deafening roar, louder than thunder, arose from the people: "Down with Compulsory Education! Down with the school!"

This speech was followed by a review of the troops, which lasted till night.

Emperor Pinocchio, tired but satisfied, then returned in state to the royal palace.

The Emperor Becomes As Black As A Crow

IT was no easy matter to be an emperor. There was a great deal of work to be done, and work was always tiresome to Pinocchio. Each day he must get out of bed at a fixed hour, and allow himself to be washed and oiled. Then came breakfast, and after that the ministers with the affairs of state.

True, his work did not seem hard. He had only to say "Yes" or "No." But in the task of deciding whether it should be "Yes" or "No" lay the real difficulty.

Sometimes he would be left with only a few servants, among them some boys to entertain him or to drive away the flies with big feather dusters, which tickled his nose and made him sneeze. These were pleasant moments in his life, but he was often bored, and being a cunning rogue he thought out a plan by which once in a while he could be freed from care.

Among the boys at the court was one who resembled him in all things except in the color of his skin. What had Pinocchio planned?

One day, while strolling through the woods near the capital, he called the boy to him and taking his arm, said to him in a gentle voice, "Do you love your emperor?"

"Is it necessary to ask, your majesty?" replied the boy, moved to tears at such an honor.

"And should you like to do your emperor a favor?"

"Your majesty, to do you a service I would go at once, with only my feather duster to protect me, and pinch a boa constrictor's tongue!"

"Good!" replied Pinocchio. "You are a fine lad, and you will become a great man. But let us put aside boa constrictors for the time. I have often been sad because I am not like my subjects. I should like to color my skin so that it would be like a native's, dear Marameho, like yours. You know how pleased the ministers would be."

"Your majesty, it would be the brightest day of our lives!"

"Good boy!" exclaimed the marionette. "If you always answer so well, I promise you the place of keeper of the king's treasures."

The boy's eyes shone.

"Well, can it be done?" asked the marionette.

"Nothing more simple, your majesty," replied Marameho. "I know of a plant, the fruit of which will serve our purpose."

"When can we get this wonderful dye?"

"To-day, if your majesty will permit me to absent myself for a short time," replied Marameho with great respect.

"Go, go at once," ordered the marionette, greatly delighted. "But wait; there is something more. We are alone and may drop our titles. Your majesty, your highness, weary me to death. Call me plain Pinocchio, and I will call you my dear Marameho."

The poor boy was overcome with all this kindness, and planting a kiss upon the point of his emperor's nose, he vanished through the trees.

The next day a proclamation was made throughout the empire. His royal and imperial highness had become as black as the blackest of his subjects. The ministers were joyous, and they celebrated this happy event with a great feast. That day they did nothing but eat and dance.

As a rule the emperor, of course, could not take part in such amusements. It was his business to sit upon the throne while the ministers and the people danced and played before him. This time, however, the ancient law was broken. Pinocchio danced like a madman the entire night, while the faithful Marameho, clothed in the emperor's garments, sat upon the throne. No one even dreamed of the exchange.

The Hippopotamus Hunt

THE next day was set aside for a hunt in honor of the young emperor, Pinocchio the First. He would have been content to stay home, but this would have been taken as a grave insult to the people.

A herd of hippopotamuses had been discovered a few miles from the capital. His ministers agreed that the emperor must go. There was nothing else for him to do.

Besides, the hunt was for scientific purposes. As Pinocchio had made known his views on schools, he could do no less than encourage this expedition, which was the only educational training allowed in the country.

The hunters, in fact, were persons of high rank, who spent their time in searching for traces of wild animals. It seemed strange to Pinocchio that these learned hunters did not study how to protect their animals, instead of trying to kill them.

"I suppose it is the custom of the country," thought the marionette.

Two hours before sunrise the leaders in the hunt, armed with bows, arrows, and javelins, stood before the royal palace waiting for the emperor. He was to ride on the back of a bull, which the prime minister held by a rope.

They were not kept waiting long. Pinocchio the First came forth with a pleasant smile upon his lips. Inwardly, he was very angry, but little did his faithful subjects suspect how he felt.

"A fine time for a king to rise!" he thought. "Am I or am I not emperor? If I am emperor, I should sleep as long as I wish, eat what I please, and do anything I like. It seems to me that I am the slave of my people rather than their ruler. Wait, my dear subjects; I will soon prove to you what stuff I am made of."

The people waited. The ministers explained to the emperor that he was to ride on the bull.

"My dear subjects, have you lost your senses?" thought the marionette. "I certainly will not ride on a bull. How long have bulls been used as horses? This beast will hurl me into the first ditch we come to. A fine regard you have for your emperor! I almost begin to believe that you want to get rid of me and have another king."

However, there was no way of escape, and he decided to do as he was told. He leaped squarely upon the bull, and calmly sat there. The bull, fortunately, did not move.

"Good beast!" said Pinocchio, somewhat encouraged, as he gave the signal to depart.

The sun was already up when they reached the river where the hunt was to take place.

Hippopotamus hunting is a very dangerous sport, but it was one that the people dearly loved.

Scouts were sent on ahead while the hunters crawled like snakes through the high, thick grass. As they neared the river, they became very careful. With their eyes fixed, their ears wide open, their spears firmly grasped, they were ready to attack at any moment.

Pinocchio pretended that he was suffering with a pain in the left foot, and slowly dropped behind the others. He had never had any great liking for the hunt. He felt annoyed that he should always have to do things that he did not enjoy. He would have stayed where he was, but the prime minister came along in search of him.

Tired of the insolence of this man, the marionette thrust back his hat with a bold sweep of his hand, as if to say, "Now I shall show you who I am, and who I was." Pinocchio then hastened toward the river, reaching the bank at the very moment when the hunters had started a large hippopotamus out of the weeds.

The huge animal tried to get away and made for the river.

"Some one must jump into the water and kill it with the javelin," said the prime minister. Nobody stirred.

Suddenly a loud voice rang through the stillness:

"I will go."

And Pinocchio, amid shouts of admiration and terror from his subjects, dived into the river and swam toward the animal.

The hippopotamus scented the enemy and turned upon him, but the nimble marionette, swimming around the great creature, grasped it by its short, thick tail.

When the beast felt itself gently pulled in this manner it began to turn round and round like a dog chasing a troublesome fly.

This performance, which was both funny and terrible, lasted for fully five minutes. During all that time Pinocchio did nothing but laugh. He did not seem to realize what would happen to him if he were clutched by those terrible jaws.

At length the animal, blind with rage, plunged below the surface of the water, leaving the marionette and the others dumbfounded.

This adventure increased tenfold the admiration of the black hunters for their emperor, although it was not wholly satisfactory to the chief cook of the royal household, who had already planned a great dinner. But Pinocchio quickly consoled him, assuring him that when it came to eating the tongue and feet of a hippopotamus, the emperor would cheerfully forego the pleasure.

The Emperor Surprises His Subjects By His Wisdom

PINOCCHIO'S power grew greater and greater. The courage shown by him in the hand-to-hand fight with the hippopotamus had made a great impression on the ministers.

The grand council, for instance, had assembled the high court of justice, which was to try a large number of important cases. The very next morning the wise and brave Pinocchio was urged to pass judgment upon the cases to be presented that day.

Pinocchio thought of playing the usual trick upon his ministers by placing Marameho in his seat; but this was an important affair, and must be attended to in person.

"Dignitaries! chamberlains! ministers! royal judges! guards! To the court!"

The persons called came forward and knelt down to kiss the earth before his majesty; then, rising, they all moved on to the court of justice.

Beneath a canopy of ostrich feathers, held aloft by a stately African, walked Pinocchio the First, Emperor and King of all the African kings. He was wrapped in a large green and red cloak covered with precious stones, that is to say, with bits of broken glass of all colors, and shining pebbles collected with great labor from the rich mines of the country.

The court was to sit in the open air. This greatly pleased Pinocchio, for the day was very beautiful. When his majesty arrived all the great crowd of people knelt and buried their heads in their hands. They did not rise till the judges were comfortably seated on the bare ground.

At a signal from the emperor the first case was called. There appeared two men, each with his head completely covered by a large bag which had in it holes for eyes and mouth. The men bowed again and again to his highness and to the court, scraping their noses along the ground. At last they stood stiff and erect like posts.

The grand chamberlain made a sign to Pinocchio, and his majesty, turning to one of the men, asked, "What brings you before the emperor's court?"

The person addressed twisted his whole body and sprinkled sand over his head. Finally he said, "There was once - "

"A king!" thought Pinocchio, "Is he going to tell a story? I, for one, should be pleased. African stories must be amusing."

"There was once an old man - a kind old man - blacker than I am, who had many sons, and I was one of them. For this reason, the old man, being my father - "

"He was his son. He reasons well," thought the marionette, but he did not move an eyelash, pretending to be all attention.

"For this reason, the old man, my father, sent me to tend his flocks. One night I arrived at the brink of the river to water the flock. There I discovered that a sheep was missing. I was heartbroken over this, and, not wishing to return home without my little sheep, I searched everywhere, but in vain. The sheep could not be found. I sat down and began to weep. Behind me was a thick cane field. Upon a rock within the field was that man, with a sheep between his knees. I rushed to the spot and shouted out to him, 'Why have you stolen my sheep?' He appeared not to hear me. 'Why have you stolen my sheep?' It was like talking to a stone. Blinded by anger, I drew nearer. When he saw me approach he arose and ran away. I hastened to my sheep and raised it from the ground, and then I saw - it horrifies me to tell it - that what I held in my hand was only the sheep's coat. The robber had eaten the rest. My sheep! My poor little sheep! I shall never see it again!"

Pinocchio was greatly touched by this pitiful tale. He had just opened his mouth to pronounce a terrible sentence upon the thief, who was standing motionless as a statue, when the minister whispered to him to listen to the other side of the story. With an angry look Pinocchio ordered the accused man to speak.

He started as if he had been roused from deep thought, gazed around, and then said in a grave, slow voice, "The sun shines - "

"What kind of speech is he going to make?" thought Pinocchio. "Is it necessary for him to say that the sun shines?"

And as the rogue went on to speak of starry skies, blue waters, and things of that sort, the marionette lost his patience and shouted, "But did you or did you not eat the sheep?"

"Your majesty," replied the man, "certainly I ate the sheep! Ask, however, who, on the day before, ate three fingers from my left hand!"

"Your majesty, I was hungry - " groaned the shepherd. "I was very hungry."

Pinocchio shuddered. "What kind of people are these? What sort of place have I fallen into? Fortunately for me I am made of wood."

Meanwhile the two had lowered their heads, waiting for their sentence. Pinocchio was too much shocked to say a word.

The grand chamberlain came to his aid and whispered something in his ear.

"Speak!" replied the marionette, "I bid you speak, for whatever you do is well done."

The minister was pleased at the faith his majesty had in him. He turned his dark face toward the two offenders and said, "One sheep and three fingers! You shall both be hanged."

Pinocchio, half-dazed, watched the minister.

Case followed case, and at the end of each one Pinocchio said to the minister, "Act. I bid you act. What you do is always well done."

The minister knew so well how to act that on this one day there were sentences amounting to five hundred years of imprisonment, and two hundred years at hard labor, while a thousand prisoners were to be lashed, and one hundred were condemned to die. Justice had been done. The emperor Pinocchio was led back to the royal palace amid the shouts of the people. He was declared to be the mildest, the wisest, and the most just of all kings, past, present, and future.

Pinocchio Travels Through The Empire

IN order that his faithful subjects might behold their new sovereign, Pinocchio the First resolved to make a tour of the villages of his vast empire and see with his own eyes the needs of his people.

The arrangements were made by the ministers of state. Messages were sent to all the governors to make preparations for the event, to select committees to meet the emperor, to provide entertainment, in short, to have everything in readiness.

It was a big task. The emperor, however, did not trouble himself about it. He amused himself watching the crickets and the birds, laughing at the antics of some little monkeys, and playing with his boy pages.

Sometimes he spoke of his past. He told his pages about his travels, his struggles, his suffering. He told them how he had struggles with the waves of a stormy sea, and about the fish from whose stomach he had rescued his father Geppetto. He recalled his dear Fatina, that gentle and beautiful lady with the blue hair, and, placing his hand upon his breast, took an oath, as emperor and king, that we would have her come to Africa. That thought made him happy, and he went on to describe the feast they would have on her arrival. He had resolved to make her queen of one of his states.

Marameho shared the joy of his emperor, but a cloud of sadness came over his face when he heard him build these castles in the air, and make such plans for the future. The poor boy had already seen too many changes to believe that anything in the world would last long. He was aware that his emperor was in grave danger, but he did not dare to warn him.

However, events quickly ran their course. The preparations were completed, and on a bright, sunny day, Pinocchio the First, Emperor and King of all the African kings, took his place upon a litter made of branches, which was borne aloft by four robust men. Following these came all the ministers, and the day's march was begun.

Wherever they went, there was loud applause for the emperor. The mothers were pleased because their ruler had promised to stop compulsory instruction. They expressed their thanks in flattering words, some of which reached the emperor's ears.

"How fine is that wooden head!" said one. "It is easy to see that he is a king of great endurance! They say he can jump wonderfully - just like a marionette!"

Toward evening the tents were erected. In the largest of these Pinocchio gave a supper to all the ministers, a splendid supper which lasted till late that night. A blazing fire protected the court against the attacks of wild animals and the cold of the night.

The ministers retired about midnight. Pinocchio, left alone, began to walk up and down in his tent, with his hands behind him and his head lowered. He had seen at school a picture of the great Napoleon in the same attitude.

He thought of his stay in Africa, and of the strange things which had befallen him. He thought of the treasures he had not yet found. While pondering on all these things he approached the entrance of the tent, and in the faint light of the dying fire, he saw a group of men huddled together. Drawing nearer, he heard them talking.

"If things go well, as I hope they will, we shall gather many presents," the prime minister was saying. "It cannot be denied that he is attractive, and I am sure that all our people will vie with each other in making gifts. Therefore, I entreat you to be patient. When the visit is ended we will share what has been gathered."

After a long silence, interrupted only by the roar of a lion prowling about, the prime minister continued: "As for him, we will dispatch him in the quickest way. If he were not of wood," he added in a deep voice, "he would be good roasted, but - "

Then some one threw an armful of branches on the fire. The flames lit up the tent, but Pinocchio saw and heard no more, for he had vanished out of sight.

At dawn, notices were sent throughout the whole country that the emperor had disappeared, and that there was no trace of him to be found! The confusion was terrible. The people everywhere were aroused, charges were brought against the government. The matter became so serious that the ministers were forced to flee.

Among those who escaped was the prime minister. He went into the forests determined to find the emperor. Having strong legs and a keen nose, he was well fitted to track any kind of animal, including a marionette.

In fact, after many hours of hard work, he beheld the emperor scampering away from a herd of wild beasts. They evidently wanted to make a meal of him. The court gentleman knew that these animals would soon give up the chase, and was content to follow at a distance. After a while daylight drove the beasts away, and the poor, tired emperor threw himself flat upon the ground to regain his breath. Scarcely had he done so when a roaring more terrible than that of wild beasts caused him to spring to his feet in the vain hope of making his escape.

Pinocchio Is Placed In A Cage

ALAS! there was the prime minister. He had caught hold of the marionette and tied a rope around his neck.

It would be impossible to describe the wrath of the poor emperor. He wanted to say a few things and to do even more, but the cruel minister struck him with a whip.

This kind of argument convinced the emperor that it was best to remain quiet.

"That is how I like to see you," said the minister, pushing Pinocchio forward, and holding him by the rope as the farmers do their donkeys on returning from market.

Thus they walked a great distance, until they came to the top of a hill from which could be seen a large tract of country covered with huts. The minister turned toward Pinocchio and spoke as follows: "My dear emperor, we must decide upon some plan of action, if we do not wish to starve. You see to what a miserable state we are reduced. We have no money, nor have we any food; in short, if we do not earn something before night, we shall not only be compelled to sleep in the open, but we shall go to bed supperless. If you were not made of wood, things would not be so hopeless, because I could eat you up and you would last some time. But since this is impossible, I have resolved to carry you around the village and place you on exhibition before the public. You will make money, do you understand? Now be good enough to give me your aid. Help me to put together a cage from the bark of these trees. We shall make money, much money!" And the minister rubbed his hands gleefully.

The marionette did not share in his joy. In fact, he was on the point of showering bitter reproaches upon this unfaithful servant, who was now going to exhibit him in the public squares, but he decided to wait for a better opportunity. Accordingly, he began to strip the bark from the trees without making any objection.

When the cage was completed, the minister turned to the marionette and said: "Enter. From now on, there shall be no more talk of emperor. I am your master, and you are my faithful slave. Forward, march!"

The command had been given in a way which made its repetition unnecessary, and Pinocchio knew that he must obey.

Pinocchio Performs For The Public

WITH the cage on his head the ex-minister walked into the village, whistling as he went to attract the attention of the people.

"P-r-r-p, p-r-r-p, p-r-r-p!"

It was a holiday, and the people flocked around him. Everybody wanted to see, everybody wanted to admire the rare animal in the cage. Shouts of wonder burst forth on all sides.

It is easy to fancy how Pinocchio felt! He longed to be a cricket, or a mouse, so that he might hide in some hole. How he wished that he were a butterfly or a bird and could fly to his home!

He stood there, huddled up in one corner of the cage, trying to present as little of his body as possible to the eager eyes of the crowd. He prayed for aid with all his heart. It was useless. The cruel master saw that the square was filled with people, eager to look at the marionette. He opened the cage, and when Pinocchio stepped out he made him run around in circles like a monkey.

Then the minister addressed the people:

"Africans of Africa! What you see here is not, as you believe, an animal; at least, it is not a wild animal. It is a boy. He is like many other boys that are to be found in certain parts of the earth. How he happened to fall into my hands would be too long a story. When I tell you about his habits and his mode of living, you will be able to judge for yourselves how strange a creature he is. Just think, on arising in the morning, he wants to wash his face, neck, and hands, and with what? Water!"

At these words, a murmur of surprise arose from the spectators, and some of the people laughed outright.

"That is not all," he continued. "When he has washed himself, he passes through his hair an object, made of bone, that has long, pointed teeth. Do you understand his purpose?"

The mothers looked at one another, and some of them touched the woolly hair of their children, glad that their little ones did not have to undergo such hardships.

"Nor is that all. You must know that when he wishes to blow his nose, he takes from his pocket a piece of linen, called a handkerchief, and blows his nose upon that."

An outburst of laughter greeted these words and completely drowned the voice of the speaker.

"But there is more, my people! This individual possesses the ability to eat raw butter, yet his meat must be cooked. He takes porridge with a spoon and caries it to his mouth. He is even stupid enough to cut bread with a weapon called a knife."

The astonishment was great! When it had subsided a little there was a rush to the huts. The people came out carrying water, raw meat, and butter. One brought a chicken, which the minister immediately killed and cooked.

At the word of command, Pinocchio washed his hands, neck, and face. This the marionette did willingly, for he felt the need of it. Then the broiled chicken was given to him. Pinocchio, to the delight of all, cut off one of the legs with his knife, and having spread it with pieces of butter, proceeded to eat it with evident relish.

The women then wished to see him comb his hair. Pinocchio, who had no comb, passed his fingers through his tangled locks, and finally succeeded in parting them. Then he drew a handkerchief from his pocket and blew his nose. The children shouted with glee, and even the parents could not help laughing at the queer things the marionette did.

Pinocchio Breaks The Cage And Makes His Escape

FOR the next few days the poor Emperor and King of all African kings was compelled to exhibit himself, and to repeat his performances before thousands of eyes eager to see his strange accomplishments. He was compelled from morning till night to hear the insults of the boys and the laughter of the men. All this made him very miserable.

What annoyed him most was the warning he received not to refuse to eat whenever food was brought to him. "That is what the monkeys and the elephants do," said the marionette sorrowfully, recalling what he and his school companions had seen when they went to the circus.

It is unnecessary to say that he thought of his father, of his dear Fatina, and of his home. They were constantly in his mind. Slowly, slowly it dawned upon him that this way of living could no longer be endured, and finally he was convinced that if he did not soon see his little home, if he did not soon eat the hard, black crust given him by the loving hands of his father, if he did not soon drink the water from his own well, he should die of a broken heart.

"My home, my home!" he cried, the tears rolling down his cheeks. "Home, my home!" he repeated, no longer thinking of the gold and silver for which he had come to Africa.

"I want to see my father again." And then he stood erect in his cage. His head went through the top of it and the side fell apart. Away he leaped over the heads of the crowd, away like lightning! Out of the village, across the plains, beyond the hills! Compared with him, the swift south wind would have seemed no faster than a snail.

He ran and ran and ran. Nor did he make an end of running until he reached the wide waters of the Mediterranean Sea.

There he stopped. He looked back at Africa, the land of all his empty dreams; then flinging himself into the water, he said aloud, "I will return when I have a little more sense."

At that moment a familiar voice shouted to him: "Good Pinocchio! Hurrah for Pinocchio!"

CPSIA information can be obtained at www.ICGtesting.com
Printed in the USA
LVOW07*2042100913

351837LV00012B/277/P